A Clue to the Invisible Pyramid

A Collection of Short Stories

Volume 1

Dr. Dee Hacking

International Bestselling Author and Bestselling Publisher

A Clue to the Invisible Pyramid

Do you like intriguing stories with a little mystery, a ghostly vibe, and a tech twist?

Welcome to **A Clue to the Invisible Pyramid**, where haunts and secrets populate this platter of mind-tingling short stories and 2-minute tales.

About the Author

Dr. Dee Hacking is a 5x International Bestselling Author, 2x International Bestselling Publisher, Ghostwriter, Doctor, Homeopathic Physician, and Clinician, running her own business for just under 30 years. At her boutique publishing house, House of Wellness Publishing, she is proudly the creator of **The New Rules of Wellness** book series of transformational stories from health experts who lead from the heart, and **SPRUIK IT!: Cultivating the Willingness to Back Yourself to Your Success**, along with fiction and non-fiction, inspirational guided journal puzzle books, and many other projects. Dee hails from metropolitan Melbourne, Australia, and lives in tropical North Queensland with her loving husband, John. Jointly, they are very proud of their three children, and currently, they have one grandchild. If you don't find Dee at her favourite coffee hangout or poolside, you will find her curled up in her plush writing nook.

DISCLAIMER

Copyright © 2024 House of Wellness Publishing.

References:
All website links provided are correct at time of first publication.

Contents

1. A Clue to the Invisible Pyramid.

I stare back at my reflection. A piece of my hair falls in my face, and I stick it back behind my ear to get a better view of myself – the lake is as clear as a mirror. My Granny stands behind me, holding the most beautiful shell I've ever seen, a conch. It resembles a pink and white spider more than a shell and is very out of place in a freshwater environment. I hold the shell up to my ear and hear Granny speaking; I blink, and she vanishes behind my shoulders. The calm sound of her voice resonates in my ears. My eyes flash open, and I realise I'm entangled in my bed sheets, my long hair wrapped around my armpit and drenched in sweat from the summer heat, choking on my saliva. It's 5.00 am, my bedside digital clock tells me. I lie there and think of Granny and that shell. I'm told I'm weird. I feel weird almost always, but strangely, my doctor says it's normal.

"It's normal to feel weird all the time?" I asked for clarification at last week's appointment.

"No, you are normal," she said, giving me a script for Celexa.

I am normal but feel weird; my friends feel weird, too. They said they feel weird in a different way; they don't have nightmares like I do, and I know they don't have to take Celexa.

"Pfft, teenagers," I often hear the adult collective sometimes spit out from between their teeth.

"Who is normal?" I asked my Granny the weekend we visited her at her beach house.

"Not too many people," she giggled.

I love that beach house! I regularly asked Granny if I could move in and live with her.

"One day!" she smiled such a sweet smile, and began her list. "Elsie down the road is normal, Jackie next door is weird, Salma is weird at Number 21, but Nancy at 46 is normal," went on Granny thoughtfully. Then she added, "You are normal, Aurora." She inhaled her cup of tea and nearly choked. "Oops, that went down my breathe hole instead of my swallow hole!" We both giggled and made her choking worse. Once she recovered, she continued, "You are a normal, sweet child with a normal life; don't let anyone tell you otherwise! You just be yourself, pet."

Now I was really confused. I knew I wasn't a normal kid, but Granny was kind, I think.

I was small for my age, an introvert. I had funny, thin-choppy hair and a crooked smile. I'd look in the mirror, and the left side of my face wouldn't smile back at me. My friends told me how special I was to live in a fancy apartment with a pool, my dining room with its small three-seater table graced with crystal chandeliers and a Blüthner baby grand piano – I guess they didn't have all that. I thought it was terrific going for a sleepover at my best friend's house; all the siblings slept in a long room, in a dorm-style setting like camping, but it was amazing to me in your own home. They all ate together at a long table and reserved their rinse water for the next washing-up event – how totally efficient and conservation-minded – I loved it all.

Elsie-down-the-road is normal, yet wielded a 'Chinese-Chopper' meat cleaver, and I saw her hacking through hard bones from my safe vantage point over the fence. I thought she was an axe murderer when I was younger, and I also noticed she had a rifle. She would get it out when the feral dingoes sniffed around her fence line. WEIRD.

Jackie-next-door to Granny is 'weird'. Wow. I thought she was the most normal person on the street. She had a beautiful garden with climbing roses that smelled so sweet, daffodils in bloom, and lavender everywhere, and she taught me how to make medicinal concoctions out of the dog roses hips that came when the flowers dropped off. She cultivated peppermint and other medicinal herbs in the garden and baked amazing things. She would have me over for afternoon muffins, and the 'cakes that flopped' flew over the fence to the palomino horse, who would run over every time the back door swung open, running towards his afternoon snacks. "Witch doctor," Granny said.

Salma-at-Number-21 – weird – had the best collection of artifacts I'd ever seen. Crystals and wooden carved elephants were directly from India from a Yogi Maharishi. Shells (conch shells), trilobites, papers with hieroglyphs, ancient Greek stones, and coins were collected from worldwide adventures. She would have me over, and we would sit for hours with her telling me amazing stories under candlelight and burning incense. "History nut and yogi," Granny said, and told me to avoid her as she would put ideas in my head.

Nancy-at-46 is 'normal' apparently. In my opinion, she is the craziest of them all! She walks around in her underwear in winter and has a bath in her backyard in an old claw-footed tub daily and in *every* season. I see her; long boobs and saggy belly, eek. I heard my father one day make remarks to Granny about how he wasn't looking forward to my Mum 'becoming like Nancy'; I sure know what he was referring to. "Her thermostat is just off," Granny told me, and too cheap to get her house plumbed. "Wait till the outhouse gets electricity," Granny said, "pigs might fly." They would all laugh when Granny said that – I had no idea about flying pigs. I think Granny is even a bit weird at times. I do look up in the sky at times – no pigs.

Last Wednesday, we travelled to the 'Far West' near Boulia for my Dad's 30-year school reunion on a friend's property. We were not used to the intense, dry heat, even Granny, and we had to drink more water to quench our thirst and get the red dirt out of our throats. We were all coughing and picking our noses – red dirt everywhere.

James was the last to arrive, and he laughed at us all. James was my cousin who worked as a farm hand and camp drafting elsewhere; he was used to the terrain and weather. He had nice big boots on, not the flip-flops we all were in. "Beachwear," James coughed out, "not made for all these rivulets of the Channel Country."

Salma had told me to look out for the Min Min lights while we were there. I'm not telling Granny about it; Mum knew it and said, "I hope that strange alien stuff doesn't affect us." I was super-excited; I hope it does. I've been praying to whoever is listening to my prayers for weeks to show me the Min Min lights.

Salma had given me a carved stone that a friend of hers gave her who travelled to Birdsville, saw the light phenomenon, and found this strange carving on the stones the next morning right where the Min Min lights had followed her to – she said she saw a pyramid. That caught my attention. I dreamed of pyramids often.

"A pyramid right there in the middle of the desert, but not like the Egyptian ones, a glass one," Salma said the friend had told her. Salma believed her, and so did I; nobody else believed.

I had told *Jackie-the-witch-doctor* what I was up to on our upcoming Far West trip, and she gave me a concoction, especially for me to drink to get me more in touch spiritually and energetically. Salma taught me how to meditate and connect energetically. I had this *alien* engraved rock artifact with its cute little design etched onto it; I was set.

James called me out. "What are you up to? You're so weird." He saw me with my concealments as he introduced me to other people at the property who were arriving. "Not the sharpest tool in the shed," he said to them and winked as he pointed to me. I smiled my half-faced smile.

As the sun was about to set, I saw a flicker of green light out of my left peripheral vision. I looked over there quickly. Nothing. Then, as I looked around, I saw a flicker of orange out of my other eye in the periphery. My head span around. Nothing. A lady was screaming over behind a caravan close to me. I ran over, and she held a stone similar to mine with the same carving on it; it was red-hot in her hand, and she dropped it, leaving a burn mark on her hand. Another man came running up; the lady was hysterical. "There were lights all around me. I felt like I couldn't breathe," she was still gasping; she continued to ramble, "I heard a loud humming in my ears; what the hell?" And I listened intently.

"What were you doing?" said the man to her, trying to calm her down.

"I was just sitting in my camping chair, meditating before happy hour drinks started," she answered him.

THAT'S IT.

I grabbed the rock that burnt her hand from the ground and discreetly walked away. She was telling the man about the rock, and he was looking around for it. I returned to our camp and sat on Mum's yoga mat. I sat. I waited. I did all that Salma told me. I rubbed my hands together and breathed in and out three times – in through my nose and out through my mouth. I put one of the carved rocks on my left knee and one on my right knee as I had dreamed at night. I imagined that I was a triangle shape with one stone at each point. Salma told me the last time I saw her, "That is a clue. Your dream holds the clues to your 'invisible pyramid'. I bet it does exist somewhere. You just have to find it."

I believed her. I had told my friends what Salma had said, and they said I was weird. I felt my body get relaxed and heavy, but not heavy on the mat; my muscles went limp inside my body, and I could feel it. Everything went quiet. I could hear a low vibrational hum. I listened. It was calming and so lovely. I felt static in the air surrounding me; my arm hair rose, and then all the hair on my body felt like little antennas all over me.

I still heard the hum.

I opened my eyes.

Nothing was there. So disappointing.

The reunion party night went well, and everyone had fun. We ate the pig-on-the-spit and a campfire cook-up, which was delicious! As I looked at the pig being rotisseried, I looked hard at its back each time it came around; there was no evidence of wings – it wasn't one of Granny's pigs, then. It must be one of the same mysterious things like Granny's elbow grease – she had told me to 'use the elbow grease' when I was to help her clean the silver one afternoon a few years ago; I could never clean those silver things as good as she could, and I could never find that elbow grease product in her cupboard.

I noticed some dancing lights not too far away in the deep darkness behind our camp. They looked like fireflies, and I followed them around for a while, darting and zipping around – super cute. The lights then seemed to be following me. Then I saw many of the lights just up ahead, a little brighter and a little bigger, then went colourful and glimmering; they looked like the Aurora Borealis I had seen in Canada two years prior, so pretty; could THIS be the Min Min lights? The lights, however, were not in the sky; they were just as brilliant, but they were in vertical columns dancing around on the ground. One would glow, then disappear and reappear in another place. I smacked into something I didn't see as I admired the lights. A second before my nose bled, the stones started to glow red-hot in my pocket, and the humming sound was intense. My hands felt around in the dark, and there seemed to be a solid structure in front of me. I continued to press my fingers and palms into the structure, and it felt cool, metallic, or even as smooth as glass; static electricity on it was zapping me ever so gently and felt like an itch, a tingle, or a tickle on my skin. The light following me was right behind me now, and it shone on the structure before me, reflecting an upside-down pyramid! It was huge. About 40 storeys high at least, and I was standing at the tip; what would be the top point of the pyramid if it was standing the right way up? It seemed to be suspended there, upside down. The humming got louder, and my hair on the yoga mat stood on end like before my nosebleed, and then I disappeared.

"Aurora!" the search party shouted. The celebration was stalled, and every attendee searched for Aurora. Mother was beside herself. "Nothin' much can be done," said the authorities, "until sunrise." But sunrise came and went, and search parties searched in grids and found nothing of me. This went on for weeks. "She has just disappeared into thin air," read the news presenter, "after a witness had seen the Min Min lights earlier in the day."

Months passed, and Mother was put on Celexa while I was gone. Everyone said Mother went weird.

Granny's neighbours got together and told her about the *Clue to the Invisible Pyramid,* the artificial concoction. Granny told Mother. Mother was numb.

"What have you all done?" Mother was irritated with the entire world. Granny told me once I returned, Mother didn't 'go bananas' as everyone said she would; she became an empty shell of her past self. At least I didn't feel weird anymore, but Mother didn't know that then.

When I returned, I couldn't believe that I had been gone for five years. Mother had aged about 25 years, Father had left altogether, my friends were at high school and looked much, much older and had a bunch of new friends, and Granny had passed away. From heartbreak, apparently; Mother decided not to talk to her anymore. Mother blamed Granny for my disappearance.

I remained the same; I looked even younger, my hair was very long and beautiful, I seemed taller, and I had a full smile when I looked in the mirror – no facial droop, no weirdness. I was told I should do modelling, and now I was also very famous. I've got a TV series deal with a mainstream production company. The news headlines presented: "The girl who disappeared and came back five years later, untouched."

Untouched.

The mystery continued, and I was not saying anything at all, nothing about the Invisible Pyramid. Only Salma, Jackie, and Mother knew; I wanted to take them there too. Mother could do with a 'touch-up', *so she doesn't end up like Nancy;* I wonder if that's why Father left. (That's what I would have thought before my Invisible Pyramid trip; now my intellect is switched on at long last, and now I understand about those 'flying pigs and elbow grease'.) James never said another derogatory remark about my tools in the shed not being so sharp; how the tables turn, he comes to me for advice these days!

I had communicated with Salma while I was missing, and with her Maharishi via meditation and energy connection. That's how all communication was – via thought. I guess she never told anyone, I told her I was all okay. I told her I would come back. She said she would tell Granny to tell Mother; I guess she did, and Mother no longer talked to Granny because of that. "All of you are so weird!" Mother had screamed down the phone in a drunken rage.

So where did I go? I don't know. How did I come back? I don't know that either. I know I was only gone for what seemed like 20 minutes. I didn't eat, and I didn't get hungry, I didn't drink anything, I didn't see anyone – strange, I know. I guess there is a place where time stands still, but my hair kept growing, and all my ailments have gone.

I do remember things; like I said, it was 20 minutes' worth. I recall I was feeling that invisible glass structure. I remember tracing my fingers along the side of one of the glass/metallic panels, my fingertips tracing out an omega-type symbol, and as my finger slid across the pattern, the track on the metal lit up bright blue. With an electric spark to it. The artifact in my pocket also lit up with that same electric blue, and I was no longer standing in the desert heat, with the sand cutting against my shins and my nose bleeding. I was in a light room full of mist, my nose stopped bleeding instantly, and the mist became very sweet-smelling – like musk sticks – and easy to breathe in. It didn't choke up my lungs like smoke; it felt cool and smooth. I felt a little dizzy for a moment, and then the feeling went away. I felt light and as if I was floating. I couldn't see anyone. I was trying to figure out what had happened but wasn't confused; I was just thinking. I could hear a sound close by, a sound like turkeys. A group of turkeys, talking and gobbling.

"HELLO?" I called out, and the turkeys went quiet.

I could see I was inside a big moving orb. I was floating, and I could see the outline of the transparent pyramid; I was no longer at the cone, I was somewhere against one side. I felt my scalp tingling, my crusty-bloody nose was now clean, and I felt very empathetic all of a sudden, not sad or like I was going to cry, but more filled with love and compassion. If love could surround you, that's what it would feel like.

I breathed in this sweet, misty air, floated, and felt my hair growing, if that makes sense. I felt my facial muscles even up across my brow and chin, and I felt that heavy muscle feeling like what I felt when I meditated, like what Salma taught me when we meditated and I spoke to her Maharishi. He chattered away. Strangely enough, I was enjoying it, I wasn't scared, and no fear was within me – I then *heard* her – I COULD HEAR SALMA AND MAHARISHI! *Hear* – like when you listen into a shell.

"HELLO SALMA?" I let out a huge whiff of that air I was breathing. I saw mist come out of my mouth and nostrils as if it was cold in my orb.

"Aurora, is that you?" she replied.

"YES, YES SALMA, I'M HERE, WHERE ARE YOU?"

"I'm at home, at 21, at the beach; where are you?"

"I'm not sure; it's beautiful here. I'm floating and can hear turkeys, like a hen-yelp and the kee-kee call."

"So strange," she replied. "Are you coming back?"

As if to her reply, I heard a different turkey sound, and in my head, it was translated to *Yes, you are free to go back anytime; you called for us, and you asked to be here!*

"I guess I am when I'm done here," I said; what did I mean by that? Was it me talking, or was it me translating something back to Salma? Who exactly knows?

It's nice not to feel weird anymore now that I have new friends to call on whenever I wish. Salma said she would tell Granny and Mother as they were worried about me.

"I won't be long," I replied, and Salma was gone.

I took another deep breath out of the sweet musk-mist as I felt I was getting a headache. The headache went away immediately, and I wondered if the mist was some kind of gaseous nutrient.

Granny suddenly sat beside me.

She faded into manifestation and sat beside me in my orb – my orb grew bigger to accommodate her.

She looked at me and hugged me. "Oh Aurora, we have been so worried about you!" she cried into my shoulder.

"Oh, Granny, why, Granny?" Musk-mist once again was rushing out of my mouth. "Where did you come from just now?" I was so surprised to see her that I was taken aback for a minute, trying to figure out if this was real; maybe I was dreaming. I did dream these sorts of things, and when I woke up, I was so disappointed that it was just a dream.

Granny just hugged me.

I felt her talking to me in my head. *Oh sweet Aurora, we have all missed you so much. Are we dead?* I still couldn't figure out if it was my thoughts or not. The turkeys got louder and louder.

No, Aurora, it's not you, it's me, Granny; what happened to you in the desert? Where are we now? What's going on? Where have you been?

Granny was looking deep into my soul through my eyes.

I told her, "I don't know, Granny, I'm here, you're there, I spoke to Salma a minute ago!" Although I felt so confused, just as much as Granny was, I was calm, content, loved, and NEW!

Yes, Salma told me you were all okay and coming back. I told your mother, and she has gone very weird.

Granny looked sad.

I told her to breathe in some of the sweet mist; it looked like she was holding her breath or not breathing at all. She did. She smiled.

Ahhhh, I see. I love you, Aurora. You return as soon as possible; everyone needs you back. I've left a gift for you at home. Granny cuddled me again, kissed me on my cheek, and faded away. *I'll see you again soon.*

I could feel those making the turkey sounds close to me, but I couldn't see them. I felt a presence. All my arm hairs stood on end. I felt static around me and heard that humming sound; this time, the hum had a vibrational sound, with an ebb sound, like a beat, but not a beat. I felt I was being ushered out somehow. *Thank you for the knowledge and information, and see you again soon*, came a voice inside my head.

My orb shrank to its original size, and my sweet mist became a bit thicker, and I felt happier. I felt a kind of gentle movement, then gravity. I felt the heaviest I had felt with my legs like weights.

I was now sitting on my bedroom floor at home in our apartment. I couldn't move. I looked around; my lungs hurt, my eyes burned, and I coughed as the last sweet mist left my body.

"HELLO?" I called out, clearing my throat, "HELLO?" Standing up, trying to get my legs to move. As I stood up, I stood on my hair; it was so long.

I searched the apartment, running from room to room. It was empty – no furniture, no gold chandeliers, no baby grand, no one was there. I went to the bathroom and looked in the mirror. The person looking back at me was me, but I looked different. A little younger but much taller. With long, thick hair and beautiful skin, my smile was straight and beaming.

I didn't feel weird anymore.

I went outside. Mother wasn't in the pool, but our neighbour in the next apartment came flying out of her front door. "OH AURORA!"

Police were called.

I hardly recognised Mother when she came an hour later, and ambulances were called for me (how many did they need for just one person? I guess it was a major emergency); that's the day I became famous.

I was filled in on the past five years. "FIVE YEARS?!" I was stunned.

Mother had moved into Granny's house when she died. Granny left the house to me, and Dad got the apartment in the divorce settlement but hadn't put it on the rental market yet.

"She KNEW you were returning, Aurora," Mother told me. "Salma knew too; apparently, she had spoken to you!" Mother said with a grimace and disbelief on her face. I said nothing.

Mother and I often sat at Granny's kitchen table, but as time passed, Mother didn't talk much. I could hear all the chitter-chatter inside Mother's head – chaos inside her head. Mother held a lot of hatred and blame towards everyone else: Granny, Salma, Father, and even ME for *destroying her life when I went missing.*

Mother says she is sick. She is on Celexa, hydroxyurea, and cladribine. I wish I could take her to the Invisible Pyramid to fix her cancer, but she won't listen to me – I won't even suggest it. She holds a darkness no one can penetrate; Salma wants me to take her. Salma even wants to go herself.

Salma and I went to the beach at the end of the road past *Nancy-at-46*; she has her bath inside the house now. As we passed *Normal-Chinese-Chopper-Elsie-down-the-road,* she waved and said she had an awesome lamb roast ready for our dinner when we returned.

The beach is amazing – calm, warm, and serenely inviting aquamarine water. Salma and I bend down and pick up some particular little rock artifacts with an omega scribed, even engraved, into them. We sit on the beach on our yoga mats, meditating and waiting. The little rocks we hold start to glow, and we can hear a low humming noise and static in the air.

We were only gone in Earth time for 30 minutes, and back in time for Elsie's lamb dinner, and it was delicious. Pyramid time was less than a minute, and Salma was super impressed that all her body ailments had 'completely gone'. It's so nice not to feel weird anymore, as I hold the conch shell up to my ear – I listen, I hear, and I smile as I listen to the voice chatting back to me.

2. Death Card.

The video clip starts with the metal grinder sparking, and as the song notes begin, a group of men sit around a table playing poker.

>*Yeah, hey-yo, I think about death a lot, when will I go, I want to make the best of life before the end of my show, cuz I have been so close to dying but I won't let my flow stop…*

My voice begins to sing in the video clip that has just gone live internationally; it's like I'm listening to a disembodied voice from some far-off vocal artist. I listen to the words like I'm listening for the first time, and a friend of mine sits next to me. He said that's his life too, and a friend on the other side of the world who had just listened to my new release also said the same thing in a message. Other pairs of ears in both the Northern Hemisphere and the Southern Hemisphere almost simultaneously, like 'a wave of powerful life-changing recognition', all resonate with my words too, unbeknownst to me…

*****

The snow in the front of the entrance was two feet deep when the sunlight broke through the next morning. Adam's jacket, which had been used to cover the floor at the door, was now frozen solid and would no doubt take a long time to thaw. Digging his way out, it was a different world outside today. Not only was everything white – snow clung to the branches, which bent as if they were with fruits laden – but the sun hit the snow in an unfamiliar way, like a glowing dazzling light. Adam's life would never be the same again. He had called himself Ken for so many years but would go back to his birth name, Adam, from now on, and he felt it.

Last night, he had woken up in a pool of blood on his cabin floor. A song was playing late on the TV, and the flickering and glowing lights issuing from the tube in the dark had sent shivers all over him. Adam had just sat there holding his now-crusty bloodied head, watching and listening…

Had Cotard delusion where I thought I was already dead, from psychotic features all up in my schizophrenic head, had psychotic episodes my mental got dark, felt like I died with every episode like Kenny from 'South Park'…

"That's my life!" Adam had voiced into the darkness. Had he just died and come back? Had he seized and passed out and hit his head? Was the knife sitting next to him used? Had his alter ego come out to play? Had he died in every episode of the term of his natural life – like Kenny in 'South Park'? Adam would never know, but today's world looked and felt very different.

He took a step forward and sank up to his thighs in the snow.

*****

Far away in tropical North Queensland, the A/C blares, set at 21 degrees Celsius. Little icy wafts come down from the oscillating vent and are received with a satisfying sigh of contentment. Today, the owner of the sigh is more content than ever, and this is not just due to the icy blast from above.

"What is that noise?" chimes in his wife from the other room.

"OHHH, come and look at this…this is totally mind-blowing!"

She pads in to find him sitting in his 'whisky chair' beside their bar, watching something on his phone.

Soul was full of sadness when I felt I don't exist, and there's just levels to the layers of the darkest loneliness, men and women dyin' in the cold from drugs and homelessness...

"Unbelievable!" He looks up at his wife as she sits beside him to watch it.

The chorus begins.

This life's worth living because I'm still alive, I'm trying to find my way in it; it's hard to survive, and I know that if it's time I should just close my eyes, in search of better days with no more hate in their eyes...

He hadn't thought until that moment, but he said it; HE knew beyond a doubt it was true…this was him too. He reached into his heart again, but this time, it had no need for brevity or coaxing – just a kind of bliss, surrender, and love that a man needs to thrive. He had made it. He made it through all those years of fraught survival, unspoken moments of duality, and furious tirades; he is still alive…more than ever.

He and his wife look at each other in relief and realisation…and cry together…

This life's worth living because I'm still alive...

*****

The Express Post package is met with excitement, and she opens the small box. It's her ring, the moon-crystal order. Her excitement is about to spill over, but then she is totally distracted by her ear being nibbled and the radio suddenly blaring. This is not the picture she had imagined in her mind – sitting with a quiet cup of coffee, opening her long-awaited package from the USA, and placing her Moon-Magic ring on her left hand (fourth digit, just to try it on, of course)! She freezes. Lyrics chime from the radio, and her fiancé sings along to them as he nibbles her ear.

*Then they took my close friend, now with God I've got a bone to pick; blood in, blood out, I'm crushing all your bones with picks, and my gun is like behind the scenes, cuz it has bonus clips; life's about choices just like a pretty woman who gets offered lots of *D*...*

"STOP!" she exclaimed, and shrugged her shoulders hard – the nibbling stopped. "STOP!"

> *This life's worth living because I'm still alive, I'm trying to find my way in it; it's hard to survive, and I know that if it's time I should just close my eyes, in search of better days with no more hate in their eyes...*

"What?" he said. "I love that song, it's a new one by Wildcard!" he added excitedly. Still stunned, she was frozen in that spot for what seemed like an eternity, holding her now-forgotten moon-crystal package; it just hung dangling from her stiff fingernails. Her eyes widened as the song went on. They stood silently. She listened. He watched her in her stony state and vacant stare.

"This song is about me," she eventually choked out. "I've got something to tell you before we get married."

*****

Theo traced his fingers through his long hair as he looked in the mirror. "I know the kind of man you are," he said to his reflection. "You take the hardest work and do not complain. You get furious with me at the worst times, but I cope and choose to thrive." He winked at himself and hightailed it out of there as he heard the sirens, wiping the blood from his fingers and wiping down the gun. Albany was smaller than Theo had expected, though the largest settlement he had seen since he had landed in Boston. Some of the streets were paved, and the grander houses, like the one he was fleeing from, were built of brick, with long eaves and square roofs. He met his pick-up boat on the Hudson River, and the small craft dodged blocks of ice that littered the river like floating boulders. He turned the radio up.

> *Simple said this beat was haunted and when he sent it to me, I'll be haunting all my beats with all my spirit when it's looming, and remember memories about my life and how it was...*

"HOLY CRAP!" Theo listened.

> *That *S* stuck with me forever, I was reaching for hope, and*

*Paps would be so *F* happy I'm not reaching for dope; I wonder if we get more tired as we get up in age, cuz God's preparing us to die at the end of our days; I always want to put out music just as much as I can before I die...*

Realisation struck as the song went on.

Just know when I finally die I hope my lyrics get played, I wanted to make you laugh and help you escape all your pain; I've lived a crazy life at times and it came equipped with lessons...

"It's you, bro!" said the boat driver, after the song had finished.

Theo's heart was changed forever in that moment. He had chosen his own urn and placed it on the mantel only last week, knowing what was coming at some stage, actually 'feeling' the burn as the bullet would pass through him, maybe at this moment – escaping his pain, and not intentionally breaking any more hearts of others, for life.

*****

The traffic on Freeway 10 was unusually quiet for this time of day. Maybe the universe knew today was the day Imogen's life changed for the better, and placing an open pathway before her on many levels was a way of celebrating the new 'ease'. Nothing felt like she had won the lottery. The engine of her blue Dodge hummed, sounding like it was purring in contentment, mirroring her current mood. She survived. Her new life was packed in the back of the Dodge, and the road ahead was the road to freedom. She found herself unconsciously singing along to the radio.

This life's worth living because I'm still alive, I'm trying to find my way in it; it's hard to survive, and I know that if it's time I should just close my eyes, in search of better days with no more hate in their eyes...

"No more hate in my eyes..." she says to her reflection in the rear-view mirror. She continues on towards Western Promises, with a broad smile on her face, and hope in her heart.

*****

I watch myself at the end of my video clip – joining the men at the poker table, sitting in my green hoodie, arms folded tightly; the metal grinder stops its sparking, and I am stood cloaked in darkness with the shining light behind me, and my white 'California' shirt discarded, muddied and laid to rest.

I hope you do not pick up the Death Card.

3. Please Return to April Baxter.

April's toes seemed to squeak as they dug into the warm sand. It felt so relaxing as the sand pressed between her toes, and her feet sank as the next set of small waves washed over her feet. With little thought, her body began moving towards the sea. She held her red sundress up out of the water and never saw the red balloon coming her way. "April! Catch it!" shouted her brother, running towards her with crazy arm gestures; she noticed a bunch of other people running behind him making similar gestures. She reached up and caught the dangling string, plucking the balloon out of the sky with a jerk and smiling, unsure what the fuss was about.

"We've been chasing it all along the beach," her brother puffed out, standing beside her, hands on knees, flattening his back out, trying to catch his breath. His running cohort fell short and copied his breath-catching technique, all puffing and panting.

The balloon resembled a kid's party balloon, just a little larger, and as April turned it around, she noticed an envelope attached to the neck via a clamp. She flipped the envelope over and found words on its front·

PLEASE RETURN TO APRIL BAXTER

"What does it say?" asked Alex. April just blinked.

"What the hell?" Alex sputtered as she showed him. "It's for YOU?"

April was puzzled, too. "It must be another April Baxter," she said. "It's not important, nothing in my life is ever important."

She gave the balloon back to Alex, and then lifted her chin to nod as he pushed the envelope into her pocket and started to run again up over Brighton Hill.

*****

The doors of the music conservatorium swung closed with a thud, then the reverse-swing caught her and nearly lifted her off her feet. It was the long-awaited release day of her 'Starry Sky' piano solos collection – already playing in her earphones on repeat more as a manifestation tool than by choice (it was making her smile with pride and self-acknowledgement of coping with all the hard times) – so she was excited, and not to be put off from that by the fright of the heavy door-swing attack. Her red jacket had caught in the door hinge and flung her backwards.

"Here, April, look what I found," said her cellist friend, running towards her with a large red balloon. "It was just floating in the air, and the envelope attached says to return it to April Baxter, so is it yours?"

April looked at him, puzzled, read the front of the envelope, and then opened it and started to read aloud from the instruction card that had been contained within.

*****

The forest was particularly cold and kind of creepy, but walking through the winter woods had that familiar muffled sound; some far-off crows were calling, and the heavy noise of my footsteps seemed to ring loud internally. Snowflakes pressed against my cheeks, the inbound snow sending my face icy, and I pulled up my scarf over my exposed red nose – maybe an afternoon walk hadn't been the smartest idea. Dude, my canine 'son', jumped up and licked at the falling snowflakes with the kind of enthusiasm that only a puppy can really get away with. The snowflakes he missed with his tongue fell on him and stood out on his dark coat, reminiscent of desiccated coconut on a chocolate cake. My own coat, my favourite red puffer jacket, made that *scrape-scrape* sound as my arms swung back and forth. I gritted my teeth, continually frustrated with myself and the world – particularly after that terrible divorce.

A large red balloon started to descend through the treetops, even more crows squawked slowly, and a far-off coyote voiced its opinion, too. The sight of the balloon stopped me; I stared at it, shivery and frozen to the spot. I think I became more frozen than my surroundings. The balloon descended further as if gingerly approaching me directly, and it came to land in front of me. I looked around – was this some kind of Stephen King 'IT' joke? My shivery feeling left, and I picked the balloon up by its string and then turned over the attached envelope. "Please return to April Baxter," it read. This MUST be some joke, and I waited for someone to pop out of the woods. There was no one, and there were no footsteps either. Silence. Just Dude and I.

"April Baxter," I repeated to myself. I had changed my name from April Baxter many years ago. Who knew me as April Baxter? No one, these days. And how would they have found me, anyway, way out here in the Canadian boonies? I opened the envelope and read the handwritten card.

*****

She slammed her foot on the brake, and the red sports car behind her performed skilful evasive manoeuvres to avoid her sudden stop. "Get off the road, you crazy woman!" the angry occupant of the sports car shouted as he accelerated away. But she had her eyes fixated on something on the side of the pavement – a red balloon seemed to be *following* her; she had noticed it for some time, always there whenever she had glanced in the rear-view mirror.

"MUM! What was that?" the kids shouted at their distracted mother.

"I don't know, babes," she answered, her voice trailing.

"MUM!" Another car screeched, and there was a second near-miss. April quickly parked and got out, with the kids in tow. The red balloon danced and pranced towards her as if it was happy to see her. Her mobile rang, and she answered immediately: "Yup, hello?"

"Ape, what's going on? Are you all right? Miranda just texted me from the back seat of your car, terrified, and saying you were all nearly in an accident just now!"

"No, she is just being dramatic again, Jen. She is a teenager; what do you expect?" April replied.

April attempted to catch the balloon string as she juggled the phone from her hand to her ear, and tried to remember to keep an eye on the kids as well. "The weirdest thing happened…ah, gotcha," she continued speaking into the phone as she turned over the envelope to read the handwritten words, "and Jen, you wouldn't believe me even if you were here to see for yourself! Now hold on a sec…" She opened the envelope, took out the old library card, read it, and started to cry, tears smearing on her phone.

"Hello? Ape, what's wrong? Ape, seriously, what's going on?"

*****

"Many parts of the world have four seasons whereby the environment changes, as do the creatures and their behaviours, and their psyche. Our life has many more seasons than four," April took a deep breath, pausing to look at the expansive auditorium, then continued. She couldn't see the many faces looking back at her for the bright stage lights, but continued as if just talking to herself in the mirror, as she had practised earlier in the day… *"and within our lives, like the environmental concerns and the creatures, we experience many changes of action, thoughts, and states of mind. However, in the many seasons we progress through, there is gold that lies beneath if you know how to address your 'within' world."*

A thunderous applause broke out.

"It's time to dig for gold within the seasons' 'mind-fields', and find something golden within our true potential. Things we crave won't come from within the tantrums, the crying, and the 'sick-of-it-all' thought

tracks. Don't worry, I've been there too – but I'm now crafting and creating a will for life. Dig for gold, not pity."

More applause and now wolf-whistling too. As she took her trademark curtsey, she saw a banner someone had made – a big red heart surrounding her name, April Baxter.

"We love you, April!" random voices shouted out.

"Oh my, I love your outfit," voiced another excited fan.

April bowed again, blew kisses to the audience, and left the stage. She almost tripped on the long red flower-embroidered lace train on her expensive gown.

*****

"Dig for gold, not pity." Eight bewildered eyes met these written words. The words after that just offered more confusion: *"I hope this helps to adjust your core and find the real collective YOU."* These same words had appeared on four cards, these same four cards had been in four envelopes, and these same four envelopes had been held and opened by four April Baxters.

*****

Picking up the lace trim, unfortunately now sliced by her high heel, her assistant said, "It's okay, April, I'll get that fixed for you. That was a great success; well done! And I've made a reservation at your favourite restaurant."

"Thank you anyway, Emily, but I'd prefer to go home and soak in the tub with some bubbles. I'm exhausted."

"Oh, okay, I'll cancel for you. See you on Monday. Let me know if I can do anything for you over the weekend!"

The cool bubbles tingled her lips and contrasted nicely with the hot soaking-tub bubble bath. She picked up a ratty old catalogue card resembling an old library due date card found in the library books from her childhood. She had found the card inside an old book when she was decluttering her library a few years back, and it brought back a memory she had forgotten all about. She was ten years old and had been standing on the trampoline in her childhood backyard. A red balloon descended and landed right at her feet in front of her. She bounced on the trampoline; the balloon rose, hovered, and then fell. She bounced again, and the balloon landed on her hand. She reached for the string and noticed this library card hanging from the clip on the balloon's neck. "Please return to April Baxter," it read. Then she had turned it over: "Dig for gold, not pity."

She studied the now 40-year-old card she held between her fingertips, making sure not to get it wet. If only she could have told her ten-year-old self what she knew now, life would have been very different, but lying there in the tub after a successful stage presentation, she was satisfied with herself. A sip of the magic of her favourite vintage Champagne, and the knowledge that what she had done earlier that morning would change so many lives, and her own – she was content. Having lived most of her life with the few words written on that card as her life motto, 'dig for gold, not pity' had turned out to be the values and air-for-change held for so many others, too.

Her other award-winning keynote presentations echoed inside her head as she soaked: *How? That's the magical question I hear you asking me. What if I asked you three questions? What is important to you – list them, and then choose two things RIGHT NOW of major importance that would change your life immediately if those things changed. What if I told you it takes 2.5 seconds to implement change – would you believe me? Just 2.5 seconds for the action potential to rewire your mind with an electrical zap that innately occurs within us all. The electrical ZAP. It's the electrical charge time to travel along our axons to its action potential into the protein particles, synapses, and receptors, and the electrical charge is ready to be fired again. Just 2.5 seconds. Within each new second, each new thought, new mindfulness, new patterns, and new gold to dig for.*

Now, list all the things you imagine yourself to be NOW, once the above changes have occurred. VOILÀ! Can you see you have just found your treasure? You can circumnavigate space and time, joy and sadness, health and ill-health – the lot."

*****

This 30-year-old April Baxter released a red balloon while she wore a red item of clothing; she attached a note (written on another library data card) intended to be delivered to her older or younger self. She penned, "Please return to April Baxter" in her own handwriting, giving April Baxter the information and energy she would need to thrive in life. She watched the red balloon rise and elevate, floating away as she stood there, wondering how far it would travel.

*****

All of the April Baxters wore essentially the colour red when they received their message balloons, and each one received the balloon at a poignant time in her life when she needed it the most. All across the world. And across a timespan of 140 years.

Every single one of the multitude of Aprils would adopt 'dig for gold, not pity' as her life motto. Each April Baxter had brown hair and green eyes, each had been a tall child for her age, and each one loved bubbles (either to drink or to soak in – sometimes it was even both at once). And they all had black Labrador retrievers.

4. Running Dog Nebula.

I live in a town called Mark's Fluke, with a population of about 250 (give and take a few births, deaths and disappearances) and few visitors. I stand in the middle of rat and mice poop as I knock down the kitchen wall, and I come across a fluke of my own. A cascade of coins suddenly falls from a hidden wall compartment, and there she is – a Lincoln Penny. I'm not a coin collector, but I heard in Indianapolis that some renovators had a similar find and cashed in a million greenbacks. A tingle overcomes me, an excitement I must have buried deeply for so many years surfaces, and I squeal. Within the energy of that very moment, my entire life changes.

Plucking up my courage for the first time and breaking off the yellow crime-scene tape, I found that the stairs to the upper level were rickety, and the 'ENTER AT YOUR OWN RISK' sign left on the wall by some grotty-snotty teenager caught my shoulder, and it bled. The attic was at nosebleed height, the ascending staircase at a ridiculous trajectory, and it needed a lot of work, but I loved it – it would become my master suite. My imagination ran wild with renovation possibilities. Three large skylights took up most of the roof space and an old telescope stood on its tripod in the middle of the room as if it was still in use. "Cute you are, and mine you shall be." I stroked the telescope and patted its 'Sky-Watcher' insignia.

The body can be a prison; the mind can also be a prison; live your truth – walk, and the way shall appear. I did walk, and my way did appear. My body and mind prisons are no longer that, and I'm now realizing my dreams. All I wanted was more freedom than my previous life ever had for me. I wanted to buy my own palace, but here we are – a renovator's delight, the walk to my way.

I'm honestly no renovator, and my ex-colleagues would no doubt be laughing at me from their ergonomic chairs in their high-rise offices and chatting in the cafeteria of the building about my pitfalls and how sorry they felt for me and how tragic my life had become (in their eyes), but room by room, I felt like I belonged on a fixer-upper show; felling walls, re-laying floors and shiplap, sourcing farm sinks and hardware, and learning how to build new stairs. I have saved the dilapidated front sign to the property – 'Mark's Fluke of Mark's Fluke' – they seem to like being repetitive around these parts! That cache of Lincoln Pennies was the rainbow in my storm. I hadn't found a coin that was actually worth a million, but these were $160,000 each, and I had a nice bunch of them for me to retire from my old life and job and fund my new existence and my dreams.

It's midnight, and I sit on the edge of my bed in my fully renovated attic room, sipping peppermint tea and about to look through the Sky-Watcher for the first time. I had found a box of accessories in the old cupboard before I dismantled it: an Observer's Moon Map with markings on it in a red pen, a Moon Filter, a Night Sky Planisphere, and a Super Plössl Eyepiece – interesting. I promised myself it would be my new hobby once my bedroom suite was completed. I'd Google what to do with all these strange-named accessories and become an astronomer in my attic!

I looked through the telescope intently, day after day, week after week, and tried to imagine who had been looking through the lens before me, from this attic and out of the massive windows. As I struggled for two days to bring that thousand-pound claw-footed tub back up my new staircase, my imagination ran wild with who had been in this room, what they were looking at, and what filled their cup. It certainly wasn't a professional astronomer as upon further Google investigation, the device and attachments were only considered hobby pieces. I doubt it was that snotty teen, either. I had also found writings that made little sense to me at this point, but no doubt, with my new hobby in full swing, I would investigate their meaning, too – some celestial and ancient Greek references.

*****

Marky Marks has lived here in Mark's Fluke since 1974; Mr. Adam Mark owned the home from 1934, and before that, in 1909 – Mr. Mark Victor David Brenner? No way! Lincoln? My name is Amelia Margaret Marks – Mark's Fluke. I was led here and destined to be here; my son's name is Mark. I can't believe the coincidence – *my* 20-year-old son Mark loves it here and said he would move in one day 'when I no longer needed the palace'! Cheeky sod! Where did all those 'Marks' go, why did they leave, and why is the town named after them?

I feel like a private investigator and cold case analyst, as I sit in my king bed with my laptop with the full moonlight shining down and hitting my plush bedcovers, and my skin still glowing from my hot bath soaking. Self-care reduces stress levels, self-care prevents people from giving up, aids in maintaining focus and refocusing, and aids with finalizing the completion of daily boosting of happiness; self-care is an activity to do deliberately in order to become ME – so I soak, I energize, I emit new vibrant energy. I change my sense and view of the world – the best two days of my life were struggling with the thousand-pound tub that's now positioned so I can look out of the skylights up at the Northern

Hemisphere stars and imagine flying high traveling from galaxy to galaxy. Then I sleep, and I dream. From the very first day of moving into this house, eating pizza, sitting on the floor, and sleeping on my camping swag those first few nights, I had strange dreams, when I'd never really been a dreamer before here. I dream of the numbers 7500 and 1787 – recurring often, I am so obsessed I put on some lottery numbers – and the names Collinder, Melotte, and Perseus. I dream of large fallen logs on long sandy beaches, and my imagination runs wild. I researched all of that too, but I have not yet found a connection.

Off to Australia. Fire twirling on Ball Bay Beach. Astronomy. Fallen logs, Southern Hemisphere lights, and the Milky Way – the most magical thing I've ever seen. I would fly there in a heartbeat if I could.

Back in Mark's Fluke, Mark was housesitting for me. "I have a big surprise when you get home, Mom," Mark said during a call. But I already knew; he had bought me a dog. Who ran into *everything*. Mark called him Collider.

Collider was the best gift anyone could have imagined. He would sit next to me while I was in the tub and sleep snuggled into me at night; he would faithfully sit so patiently while I looked through the telescope, made my notes, and my nocturnal investigations on the laptop, night after night for months and months. No other visitors, no pestering colleagues, no stress at all.

One night in the heat of July, Mark came to visit; Collider was there whimpering, sitting next to the telescope, sitting on my maps. I was gone. The weeks followed, and the months passed; the police came and went, investigators came and went, and my 'disappearance' went cold. One night, I watched as Mark picked up my notebook and began to read the 350 pages, got out my maps and research – soon, he would realize it all would make sense to him. I watched him over the years enjoy my renovated loft as much as I did, too, patted the Sky-Watcher and talked to it: "Cute you are, and mine you shall be." And it was only a matter of time until he would figure it all out and join me. I watched him grieve the loss of Collider, I watched him get married and have his own little 'Mark's twins' running around. I would see him pick up a picture of me and call me Grammy – I enjoyed knowing my grandchildren knew me, even by proxy. I exist on 'this side' with all the other Marks from Mark's Fluke – and then I witnessed the lightbulb moment when *my Mark* awoke and joined me.

He was looking through the Sky-Watcher after a beating from his wife of now-20 years: "That damn thing!" She totally hated the telescope and all my 'crazy writings' (maybe she intuitively knew that it would exactly be the vehicle for his passage out of there?). He changed out the lens and started watching what sounded like many TV channels all at once. He went from room to room, turning off and unplugging all the electrical items in the house, frantically grabbing the remote controls and throwing them at the walls – just as I had done so many years prior. The TVs wouldn't turn off, and my body was shaking with anger and frustration, totally trembling, and I crushed the remote control I had in my hand. I dropped it with the shock of my own strength as I watched him now and the remote pieces scattered on the floor. He stood at the telescope and looked through it, seeing the Running Dog Nebula – *home, in the Milky Way*. I instantly felt I was looking at my long-forgotten home – the Heart Nebula, 7,500 light-years away from Earth. Discovered by William Herschel in 1787, it consists of glowing ionized hydrogen gas and dark dust lines, located in the constellation Cassiopeia in the Perseus Arm of the Milky Way Galaxy. Collinder and Melotte are both locations where my ancestral energy resides in atomic form. My many notes on my maps are in blue pen, not red like the last 'Mark' who wrote on the maps and noted all my 'knowledge' of 'home'. *My Mark* simply awoke; the TV signals were us all communicating and connecting with him in a way that his brain would receive and understand in its human form. And as he looked through the Sky-Watcher, he simply 'awoke' and we embraced him 'on this side' in energy form. He now realizes the answer to, "How did I get from where I am to where I really want to be?" To be happy, content, and balanced in all areas of his life? Human experiences! And he now looks back at Earth and watches his wife and kids grow up in the Mark's Fluke family home, awaiting the next Mark to awaken from the Earth-slumber experience.

5. The Line.

I see trees of green, red roses too; I see them bloom, for me and you, and I think to myself, 'What a wonderful world.'

The song trailed off. My daily morning song became the theme of my life, my meditation – Louis Armstrong is still my favourite, and yes, what a wonderful world I am in; a newly created 'false' world that has become the new norm, at The Line.

"Lovely fluffy clouds today," mentioned a fellow resident as he passed on his morning walk along the promenade.

"Yes, bulky, but fluffy today and very close too; I feel I could touch them," I smiled back.

"For sure. Have a great day, Dunns!" he puffed out.

It was 5.00 am, and just after sunrise, a sudden chill caught my skin as the sun rose, as if the life was sucked out of the world in one second. The sun gave birth to the heat of the new day – desert-dwelling was quite peculiar. I was sitting amongst the trees of green and the red roses, all smelling so sweet.

Officially, I'm a desert-dweller, although I've not felt the desert sands in years. But I watch them change daily, the shimmery horizon and the strange light bending and the refraction of the mirages. I live in a city called The Line – a linear city built in a straight line but with a vertical construction. With a capacity of nine million residents, we are nearly at that limit. My city is a two-skyscraper megastructure that runs 170 km through the desert to the mountain range at the north end. Each structure runs alongside and functions on 100% renewable energy. We also have plenty of renewable water; we even have ponds and lakes inside the city, with zero carbon emissions, and even a beach and hiking trails.

There are no cars or streets, and we have playgrounds and parks, shopping and leisure sites. Our apartments are arranged horizontally. They are roomy and ornate, and have tons of light. My sunrise bliss is on the rooftop promenade, and I don't miss a day. I work on the high-speed rail system daily, grab coffee from my favourite café stand, and live each day in bliss. I dine at my community's restaurants on a Friday night with my friends, which is a far cry from the filth of New York.

I travel the length of the city once a week; it only takes twenty minutes to each end, so I make a forty-minute round trip to keep my finger on the pulse and talk to communities in person. I have a personal pool and a gym, and I can dine out or get 'room service' if I fancy, and all the necessities of a regular city. Our priority is an urban living space where human needs are met, both mental and physical. We even have a sunroom called The Gallery, fresh vitamin D on our skin, and a garden along the entire rooftop of the city.

There is a lot of green space and internal hanging gardens in each of the forty-two communities, and there are no more dysfunctional cities where nature is second best. These are designed to enhance and protect nature and provide a functional space for coexisting peacefully. Living spaces are designed as 3D individual communities structured along the linear gradient. All services needed are within five minutes of walking distance for all the residents, such as unique communities. Each self-contained community has its own medical services and schools, and residents and visitors can move around the city and communities as they would in traditional cities. The two 'ends' of The Line are the sites for agricultural and industrial areas and tourist attractions with conventional stations. The Southern Station is called Old New York, and the Northern Station is New Sydney; both stations are themed with iconic landmarks from the original namesake locations.

A key feature here is that the 'gated communities' are secured and operated with retinal IDs for the residents. And the only things we don't have are bowling alleys and pets. Instead of pets, older adults and kids prefer the Moflins and EnoBot Smart Companions. Personally, I don't care for the pet-substitutes. I had a dog when I was younger, but he was long since passed by the time I came to The Line (I had his ashes turned into precious stones and set in earrings, which I do have here with me and wear often, so I guess in a way I found a loophole to the 'no pet' rule). As for the bowling alleys, VR ones will have to suffice, along with the VR driving range and car racing.

I call it my city. I am April Baxter, the mayor, also known as Dunns. I was called Dunce at school, and one genius prodigy-bully, Eric, called me 'Dunns the Dunce', and a variation of that stuck. I don't mind being called Dunns.

Even as I watch the fluffy clouds and the magnificent sunrise, I frown, thinking of my day ahead. I am quietly sitting here in sunrise peace, 'my time'. I can't stop thinking about all those applications I need to sift through – dealing with the sheer numbers of applications to live here has been exhausting. It has been difficult to sift through to find the most suitable residents and those who can afford to live here in an elite society. Still, we have reached total capacity at The Line, so another city, Line 2, is being constructed. The Sphere, a new site and design, is taking its first residents. That old school bully from my hometown in Sydney who coined the name Dunce for me took the mayor's position at The Sphere, so I guess he will speak to 'Dunce' again soon.

"Looks like rain, Dunns?" said my neighbour, passing by on her daily jog. I nodded back.

Regular rain has been minimal in the desert over the past nine years, but the array of irrigation systems keeps the trees and plants and flowers perfectly. Such a pretty promenade that you wouldn't know you were on top of a megastructure in a desert if you were just sitting here and looking around at the flowering orchids, roses, alpine trees, and palms.

I spend post-sunrise each morning in The Gallery sipping my herbal tea, stretching, and witnessing the dawn sparkle of each day across the dunes; my particular time, on repeat. Through the many glazed-glass window walls, I can see out the other side of the city, as it is 200 m wide, embodied in a mirrored glass façade. I have seen photos taken from out in the dunes; it's awe-inspiring, as if a wall of mirrors reflects desert dunes as far as the horizon can see. We never venture out into the dunes, and the change is too dramatic from the temperately controlled environment within the city; as a society, we are getting sensitive and refined, or 'advancing' as a race, in my opinion.

Up 'my end' of The Line, helicopter flights on the Section 42 rooftop are daily. Section 42 also has our designated 5-star hotel.

As the mayor, I have developed community events, a marathon event, and 'Walk The Line'. There is a footpath/exercise path around the fourth level, and the winner will win a cruise to a far-off destination!

At the other end of the day, the desert sun sets on the rooftop garden above my community, Section 5, named Chervil (every community is named after a medicinal herb). We are 500 m tall and offer a fantastic vantage point; the microclimate has natural ventilation, total AI organisation, and automation.

Entry to the city is via rooftop only; there are no lower-level doors, only odd service hatches for maintenance and repairs, designed to keep out any insurgents and prevent the previous desert-dwellers from enacting revenge and reclaiming their ancestral lands.

As I sat one day in my Chervil community rooftop garden, I could see a glint shining from the mountains. I looked out with my telescope and saw a set of binoculars looking back at me. I alerted my security team, and they sent a drone to investigate.

"Report pending, Dunns, over and out," bellowed the head of security in my earpiece.

We host the Eliot Games World Champion Event year after year, and Riot Games sponsors our city, a major drawcard to hosting world events; I am glad our Hotel 42 is a 2,000-room hotel. Our elongated, endless, and floating pool also hosts Olympic meets.

"You up for an espresso before work today?" blurted the A-Fin, an AI-powered intercom bot.

"Make it a long black today; I think I'm going to need it," I replied to the voice. "I'll be out in five!"

I have always loved coffee and chatting with friends no matter what time of day, something I have never had time for in New York or back home in Sydney – no more 80-hour working weeks and zero downtime. Things can just wait; it's taken me 30 years to learn that life was pleasant here.

I walked out to my front porch and was greeted with a hug and a smile. "What a magical day!" said Audrey, my PA, as she sat with Banny, my daughter, at my new designer acrylic outdoor table and chairs (that was the only covenant from the Strata Management Bot – to feature all matching acrylic outdoor wear inside).

Our security is state of the art with facial recognition and is internally regulated, with an elite-trained team to then deal with 'personalities'; I guess Big Brother is watching all the time. It's one of the application details each resident signs and agrees to in their initial purchase contract; lucky to say we have no crime.

A few things are outlawed here, one of which is throwing ANYTHING outside the Throwing Fields, netted areas for this exact activity. New residents sign a 'glass clause', and no birds.

My city has a pulse; I plug into it and FEEL my environment. This 'insane project' was based on 'blind faith in the power of technology to solve humanity's problems' (as one scholar involved with the design had put it). Solve it, it did.

Humanity problems: Liveability, environmental crisis, nutrition, crime/safety, and newly formed ideas for architecture and construction.

Architects during those years created extreme images of the future and society, and the role of architecture became the driving force by leading a team of the brightest minds in architecture, engineering, and construction to make the idea of building upward a reality.

Over the years of living in The Line, a few surprise occurrences of human interaction have developed, eliciting horrified reactions: photophobia to lighting, cabin fever, and 'perfect life' (the malaise that comes with having nothing to strive for anymore). We hadn't predicted that The Line would start to function independently from the rest of the world late, and the partition sign was to have its currency, with no need for traditional money.

Even after what feels like a few short years, nine now, it seems to be us against the world; we are 'The Line People'. My daughter and I have always said that Us-Against-The-World is our life's motto, and she will now take over the mayoral role by the time The Line votes. I plan to continue to write as a novelist and live here with her. It's an in-house publishing company, and I have up to nine million in my niche market, so I suppose it's getting more like a private community each day.

We now have actors and a production company for which a few Hollywoodites have hired rooms in our Hotel 42 to stay while filming here; many applications from them to purchase but all have been denied; the intention was not to have such an 'elite community', just a unique residence and city.

My front porch is beautiful, and I have my comfy set of acrylic chairs, and I watch the residents go by. I have gorgeous reclaimed tile from an old bank not far from my old New York home, and a friend came to visit me a few years ago; she was 'choppered in with gifts' and we spent the next week accommodating this unique tile on my front porch space. We sat there eating my favourite one-pan Tuscan chicken and drinking a bottle of the best whisky we ordered to be hand-delivered from The Line Distillery down at the Old New York section.

That was the best week I can recall having here. We etched into two tiles, her name and my name, and my daughter Banny, three exceptional tiles with special memories. Banny and her new husband think it's all adorable.

"Our residence is unique now," said Banny.

She and Jake live on our third level. I purchased the two apartments below and put them on a spiral staircase to connect them.

"Dunns," Amy had said the last time she visited The Line from New York, "your shout!" Amy loved The Line Distillery double-barrel whisky. I'm more of a bubbles drinker. Amy is flying in as we speak with a bottle of my favourite bubbles and, no doubt, a bunch of red roses.

"Susan Cochran and her daughter Phoenix, from Sorrell, are missing!" blurted Audrey.

My thoughts of Amy visiting were interrupted, and Audrey continued reading from her device.

"Susan from 'Cochran Soul' – I love her readings and numerology! Poor Susan."

"Yeh, Josh, her husband, moved from Sorrell to Casia, up your end. He moved in with his family friend. Do you know that photographer who moved from Cayenne to Casia?"

Audrey replied, "On this magical bulky-cloud-long-black-coffee-morning, it's turning into a shit-show."

"How are they affording all this purchasing and moving?" I wondered.

Most people at The Line are self-funded and now living their best life, no longer needing to 'work' their traditional jobs of the past. They have set up a life they want to live; that's half the lure of The Line: it's a 'your best life' scenario. Most self-employed residents work online or are staffers of The Line Corp, local businesses, local services, and maintenance.

"Yeh, guess she didn't see it coming," choked out Audrey. "Most psychics don't see their own business going on; how's she coping, I wonder?"

"Disappearing is one mean feat around here! I'll get security onto it."

"Already have."

"Top job, Aud!"

"Where was Phoenix last seen, do you know? And what about Susan, what's she been up to since the split?"

"Under the winding staircase at the Hyssop Waterhole, where the rocks are jutting out and you can jump in. She was there with her father Josh and some little friends; Phoenix just vanished." Audrey continued to read from the MIT tool. "Josh went missing too a couple of years ago but was found by a security drone, hidden in the canyon wall. Nice quiet family other than that. Miracle to get pregnant, the first baby was born with an extreme case of photophobia. That baby died, but Josh was secretly accused of killing him."

Audrey hardly stopped to breathe; she was riveted to the story. "Susan previously attempted to end her life after that." Audrey was still reading the updated profile. "Phoenix was born, brought them back together, and they were happy until a few months ago. Phoenix was hanging out quite a bit near the Hyssop."

"Get me the report from MuleSoft's IR drone footage, Audrey. They can't just go missing."

"The mainland has heard about the True Crime Show Documentary and is sending in a reporter with the next chopper. Josh Cochran has an ugly past that evaded our screening!"

"Shit, that will be the one Amy is on!"

"Is Josh in custody?"

"Security is at 6-Casia and is bringing both men in for questioning," Aud replied with a worried face.

"Goodness, first the mountain defection, now this disappearance – this is NOT good for us. I've just listed three twelve-million-dollar residences for sale with the global market at both Chilli and Clove private residences." I continued to frown. This was turning out to be a total nightmare. Last month, it was the mountain defection, now a disappearance in an AI city.

DRONE OPERATIONS REPORT

1. Invasion of privacy complaint: Rejected Level 1; 6-Casia.

2. Hyssop Waterhole 0900: Four young females entered the water of the waterhole. Only three subsequently exited the pool. Adult male in attendance. Security drone aerial surveying.

3. Security breach: Lower-level wall ground-level service hatches opened.

4. Unidentified mass: Triangular in nature – an upside-down triangle, light refraction, clarity, and negative space.

"Aud, get the map stitching in 3D for Hyssop from security," I coughed out, choking on my third cup of coffee. There had to be an answer. "Fetch me the security breach report for the service hatches, too – STAT, and send a foot team to the unidentified mass."

"Roger, Dunns."

The day they had to come was a month ago. The day some long-term residents wanted to explore the desert. The fantastic mountain vista views out the northern end of The Line were too good to just look at. Some young residents with their drones sent out an away team only a few months ago to the mountains, and a group of ten young men had defected to the mountains, no doubt the ones looking back at us with their binoculars that I see through my telescope. The Dunes Gang – they were rogues, and up to something.

"The helicopter has arrived; I'll send Amy to your residence so she can relax. I'll order her favourite sushi, greet the media personally, and tell them you are too busy. I've got this, Dunns," and Audrey nodded without me having to say anything. She was on automation, too, a brilliant young woman.

"You are too good to me, Aud!"

I popped on my new set of visual and audio AR-comm-glasses, pushed the button at my right temple, and called Amy: "Hey, babe!" In my visor I could see her long red hair, wild from the helicopter wind, as she came down from the roof helipad and answered, "I hear you have a drama on-site!"

"Yeh, a bit of a nightmare here!" I scoffed. "I'll see you tonight."

"A-OK babe, oh look at you, I love your new suit, Ca'zinc, is it? Very ethical!" She ended the call – or it dropped out as she spoke.

My next call was from Aud. "Tactical and Medics have been sent to the helo pad. Dunns…you need to be sitting down… The helicopter just exploded on the roof, and all personnel on the rooftop are assumed deceased; it's bad…"

I went numb. "Amy...?" I whispered in question to Audrey.

"We…believe so…and…" Aud trailed off.

I heard nothing more and dropped to the ground.

> *I see trees of green, red roses too; I see them bloom, for me and you, and I think to myself, 'What a wonderful world.'*
> *I see skies of blue, and clouds of white.*
> *The bright, blessed day; the dark, sacred night, and I think to myself, 'What a wonderful world.'*
> *The colours of the rainbow, so pretty in the sky; are also on the faces of people going by. I see friends shaking hands, saying 'How do you do?' They're really saying, 'I love you.'*
> *I hear babies cry; I watch them grow. They'll learn much more than I'll ever know. And I think to myself, 'What a wonderful world…'*

The following day, I needed to be functional, even with my heart ripped out. All personnel deceased, helipad destroyed, and a chain of events blasted off. Thousands of people were relying on me, especially to find out who the terrorists were and how Susan Cochran and Phoenix had gone missing.

"Dunns, Eric-the-bully from The Sphere is on AR comms."

"ARGHHH, SERIOUSLY?" I winced, already feeling the pain. Then: "Good morning, Eric; how can I assist?"

"DUNCE, nice day here in the tropics; how's the desert?" He gave me no time to answer: "You won't believe who I have arrested on my end – are you missing some residents?"

"Yes, why?"

"Dunce, I don't know what you have going on over there, but my helipad is down and destroyed by terrorist activity. Apparently yours too, but we also have a teenager named Phoenix in my never-used lock-up, and a cadaver identified as Susan Cochran. Your Line people, and two of my residents are missing, literally, MIA –" Eric continued, not taking a breath, "and I have drone security footage of what looks like a portal, or portal paradox, opening and closing in our canyon space."

I froze.

"Foot team to Dunns!" blared from the A-Fin.

"Hold that, Eric…Dunns to foot team, go ahead."

"Seems to be an unstable mass, kind of a portal, then it goes black and folds in on itself, repeats every eight minutes; foot team over."

"I think we have something similar on this end, Eric; so what do we do? You are the prodigy with the dark matter."

*****

Eric sat with great pride and satisfaction in his residence, which was high in his spherical cap. He had eliminated the 'whirring' noises The Sphere originally made as it would spin so slowly that no one noticed. The hemisphere of this sphere was continually generated as a device with enough energy to have its stable portals open for eight continuous minutes without muscle paralysis or flaccidity for those being transported. Offering minor distractions here and there at his own Sphere-people's expense was a price he had to pay. "Elite society, no way, Dunns," he laughed as he spoke to her on the A-Fin.

*****

Under the winding staircase at the Hyssop Waterhole, where the rocks are jutting out, if you jump in the water in just the right place, you can see a mostly hidden dry natural shelf. There's just enough room on the shelf to lay a baby down, well wrapped up against inadvertent splashes, and with a shroud over its eyes. A dark hole sometimes opens there in the canyon wall, behind the natural shelf, strategically outside the view of the security drone.

With its Sphere-people cohort, the Dunes Gang entered via the ground-level service hatch undetected this time and made their way to the canyon. The Sphere people exited The Line and were transported back to The Sphere via a shrouded portal with Human-centric Worth Tabs and the photophobic babies.

*****

Susan Cochran's body was transported back to The Line. Phoenix Cochran was sent to medical and then transported back with no memory of any incident and no memory of her mother; she was blissfully sipping her freshly brewed coffee. "Good morning, Dunns, what's up?"

*****

I sat on the rooftop, staring at the sky, getting some air, thinking of Amy, without any bliss. There were lovely fluffy clouds today, too far away to touch them. A red balloon descended from nowhere (it was almost exactly the same colour as the scarf I was wearing, funny). I reached for its string, which had an envelope attached to it, so peculiar…
PLEASE RETURN TO APRIL BAXTER

6. The Moon Bridge.

I had recently been finding that nothing really inspired me anymore. To me, it seemed simple. To let the light in, one needs many inspiring stories. Words of inspiration can let the light in, a hug can let the light in, a random act of kindness can let the light in, and knowing you are a small fish in a big pond but there is love and support around you can let the light in. I had ended up with all of this, then none of this.

I sat under a tree in the heat of the day, and I started reading 'The Cat Who Ate Danish Modern' by Lilian Jackson Braun. I had read and liked other Braun books – cat stories in fictional scenarios – so this one sounded good to me. The leading character, Jim, was not overly impressed with his new assignment. *I feel the same, Jim!* I became lost in the story and read on and on, admiring Jim's Siamese cat, Koko, who was brilliant at finding out things about a clever murder by sniffing at furniture and pawing at clues in a dictionary, so that Jim became a sleuth by proxy. *I'm really enjoying this book!*

Eventually I looked up and it was nearly sunset. The heat of the day had gone. I saw a Siamese cat slinking past me. "Koko?" I said to the passer-by beauty, and the cat turned her head and looked intently at me. *Wait, no way!* Sometimes my imagination was too strong.

My days had recently become darker and darker, my light of ambition was extinguished, and each pore of happiness was empty. My job had become redundant due to the global crisis, and an eviction notice was served on me as I was told the owners were moving back into my apartment. I saw myself penniless and homeless before too long if something didn't change. The summer after I graduated from university I had started to miss regular reading. During school I'd had less personal choice about literature, but afterwards, in spite of ample reading material of all kinds, I had chosen to be career-focussed instead and became even too busy to eat, so reading went to the dogs. No time for my particular interests. The last course I had taken was an independent study where one of my professors and I had built the curriculum together. I was inspired then. I had learned all about the genre of 'murder mystery' and even created some ideas of my own. I'd had so many things going on in my brain, before I killed all my brain cells by my choices.

The Siamese cat was still nearby, and now she came right up to me and purred at my feet. "Hello, little girl," I purred back. I figured that if I ever had a cat of my own I'd name her Braun. I imagined that she would be set in her ways, like me. I imagined her to be intelligent and humorous, like me…well, like I used to be. Our little existence would be cosy and fun. I liked the thought of that.

The sunset was fading and the stars started to twinkle.

I had sat here under this sprawling tree next to the big arched bridge so often that it felt like home. Passers-by would nod at me and even say Hi, familiar faces on their walks; it was like we knew each other without knowing each other at all. The Stone Garden Bridge was a popular place for walkers and other exercisers, and was quite a spectacular sight, as it spanned a large and beautiful pond. The Stone Garden Bridge was more casually and affectionately known as the Moon Bridge, but I wasn't sure why. It was a very high stone arch, bricks immaculately laid, very pretty. I had walked here most mornings before work, then lately I would leave the apartment to sit and read under this tree, now that I had found space and time for reading again. So much more enjoyable out in nature, too.

A wise colleague had reminded me, on my last day at the advertising office, of a very valuable thing. Her 'thought of the day' that went onto her socials was referencing 'getting out of your own way' and in our industry of personal development and advertising, that very line often popped up. "Get out of your own way, and just get it done!" But that now ex-colleague (who happened to go by me tonight during her evening run), had mentioned a vital component which resonated with me and finally the penny dropped now that I had more mental space to think clearly: "You are far too smart and valuable to be the only thing standing in your way." MY GOODNESS, that's RIGHT. I had asked myself often, "What else can I be doing towards my own success, and the success of those around me and that work with me?" So I had planned, I had devised, I had had a great morning routine, evening routine, and exercise regimen (adapted from the rehab from when I had fractured my leg when younger). I had meditated twice daily, I'd had coaches I worked with after school (as one of my business coaches liked to say, "Even coaches need coaches," and he was right), I brainstormed, I journalled, and then worked hard daily...and for what? To be made redundant and homeless. But NOW, do I get out of my own way? Well, maybe!

I had finished 'The Cat Who Ate Danish Modern', and the Siamese cat from reality, who apparently wanted to be good friends, was now snuggled comfortably in my lap and was purring. "Koko?" I ventured again, and she purred louder. I stroked her neck and back, noting that she was clearly not a stray, being healthy and in great condition.

** What are you doing out here in the park at night alone?

Wait, am I dreaming? So many busy thoughts were now running through my head. What seemed to be far-off dreams and goals and the bucket-list items, were MORE attainable than we think if we move past ourselves. I didn't want to call it procrastinating, because I knew I wasn't a procrastinator and never have been; I'm actually a woman of great action (often too much action and enthusiasm). It wasn't even about 'me not being me' as I'm very authentically me, simply doing first what one doesn't really want to do, or that one has been putting off – make time for

ME, cancel things, free up some down-time…

    ** Getting out of your own way.

I froze. *Was Koko talking to me?*

    ** Sometimes you don't even believe your own thoughts.

It's a good rule of thumb to not beat yourself up and be so stressed that you can't think (or eat, work, or remember that cats can't talk). I knew this in theory but as I sat under the tree with blinding and immediate flashes of realisation and multitudes of other thoughts crashing around inside my head, I wondered what I needed to do to bring myself to ground enough to make some sense of it all, and discover how to grow from it. One of the crashing thoughts manifested as a memory, and I recalled that a good friend of mine had told me years ago that she used to start each day by choosing a card. When she was a small child, she and her mother Marie would each choose a tarot card daily and read the little messages to each other, and wish each other a magical day. My friend had shown me her family tarot deck, a precious keepsake from her grandmother, and she and I had subsequently exchanged cards many times. I had found the ritual soothing and often inspirational, and had drawn a light energy from it, but it had become like so many other things in my 'former' life – I had lost it when I had let myself get in the way of it. I recalled now that I had been particularly inspired whenever I had drawn the Magician card, with its message of tapping into your own full potential rather than holding back, especially when there was a need to transform something. Or someone. I realised, and felt, that I needed to live by this light energy again. I had lost my way.

As I sat remembering, and analysing the message from the Magician card in my mind, I thought, *I'M LISTENING!* It looked like Koko was listening, too, and I felt as if she could hear my mind's chatter.

I thought about how the Magician has all the elements in front of him, embracing the Jungian belief of intuition, feelings, thinking and sensation with everything he needs to succeed, and is well connected. He stands upon a rich garden filled with flourishing flowering plants. His clothing depicts his purposeful activity, pure intentions and aspirations with infinity of spirit and manner. And then, I had more and more flashes of realisation, and I felt such gratitude for this inspirational energy. I spoke out loud: "TONIGHT, TONIGHT I ENTER WITH THE ENERGY OF THE MAGICIAN, AND THE LIGHT!" I received and embraced the message being presented to me, and it also seemed like I could feel my friend, who had originally gifted me the encouragement to pursue this energy, sending me her support and love too. I accepted, embraced, grew – it all made so much sense now, and my soul rejoiced in the light.

Koko meowed.

I looked down at her, and I *felt different.*

Koko jumped off my lap and walked towards the pond, and I got up and followed her. The Moon Bridge was now illuminated with what seemed like a million lights. I had never been here at night before – how magnificent, and the lights were arced and their reflection in the water resembled a crescent moon on the still surface of the pond. The night was silent and I hadn't seen another person for hours; it seemed like I might be the only human being in the world. And for all I knew, Koko was the only cat.

"Meow!" went Koko again. "I know!" I replied to her, and she and I peered into the water.

Above us the stars twinkled so brilliantly, the moon shone brightly, high in the sky, and the reflecting crescent 'moon' of the Moon Bridge lights in the water made it seem like I was suddenly living in a fairy tale. I felt like I was flourishing, like I had transformed, had become spirited and inspired. "So pretty!" Koko made a long "Meeeooow!" in reply. Now I felt like I could TOUCH the magic, like the Magician card had depicted. I blinked and double-blinked, looking into the water, where I could now see a whole city of lights in the pond. And another cat's reflection was looking back at us, but as if from under the water – not a Siamese cat, another one – and another person was looking back at me; surely not my reflection, but that of another. I tried to 'trick' the reflection by pulling away and looking back quickly. But both reflections leaned forward *towards us* so as not to lose sight of us. I looked up to see where all the 'city lights' might be reflecting from, but now there was just darkness in the night sky. I looked back in confusion, and Koko was still intently staring, too.

The strange reflections were now beckoning to us to come into the water and follow them. I suddenly felt dizzy, losing my balance and falling and taking Koko with me as I unintentionally caught her body with my foot. There was no splash. The water wasn't even cold, just buoyant. But then I felt myself sinking, and I couldn't fight or even just stop myself from drifting down. And Koko was *swimming* down there beside me to keep up with me, and then there was nothing getting in our way towards those dazzling city lights under the reflection of the Moon Bridge.

*****

A young man sat under the sprawling tree next to the Moon Bridge, with a large tour group before him. He had led this tour many times, but today felt a little different. He held a book and read to the crowd. The heat of the day was leaving and the dusk stars were starting to appear. He looked up and around at the crowd and said, "Soon you will be able to see the Moon Bridge's night-time reflection in the pond." He paused. "This is the exact spot where the woman and the Siamese cat went missing…"

He bowed his head briefly, then took a deep breath and continued, "And if you look into the water when the stars shine bright, you may see the twinkling lights of the city too."

7. You're Next!

Big Tony York said the new baby was a legend. He was never going to be any trouble, was always smiling, and was going to be easy to parent. It was alright for Big Tony to say – he wasn't the father. Amy York said the new baby was a superhero, a true miracle. He was blessed and would be the answer to all their prayers. It was OK for her to say – she wasn't his mother and didn't have to look after him either.

The baby's middle finger would zap you every time you went near him, so we put mittens on him. That was my decision. I wasn't his mother either, but I was elected to look after him. We all decided to 'keep it in the family' to parent him; everyone in this small mountain town would keep their mouths shut, and no one would know the difference. His mother died while giving birth to him; she suffered horrendous burns 'around her hoo-ha' as we were told, and died from those burns a few days later. No one knew who the father was, definitely no one from around here, or we would have known him. He was our miracle and savior, just like Amy said. She is my cousin. I am Darlene.

The baby grew nicely and became a good little boy.

He would point his little electric finger to a set of numbers; those turned out to be the correct lottery numbers, and we all became rich, thanks to him. We called him Sparky York. It was an honor to be his replacement mother, and profitable too. We never gave him another name, Sparky just stuck. Sparky York he answered to when called on the school roll, on his apprenticeship card, and we forged a birth certificate so he could get his driver's license.

Sparky was easy to parent, Big Tony was right in that respect. He looked after the other town kids on the school bus, stood up for the girls against the other mean boys, and even zapped them, issuing a nasty burn when they became unruly.

"Keep your zappy-boy away from my Alex!" yelled the nasty new lady who moved in down the street. She won't stick around long when the Yorks run her out of town. They never stay for long, these out-of-towners. They buy pieces of land and want to build log cabins on them to have 'a quiet life in the mountains.' Ha, did we have them fooled? Big Tony York lives at number 1, Amy York lives at number 3, and Sparky and I, along with my new husband, now live at number 5. We bought the whole street after we continued to 'come into all the money.' We didn't tell people how we became so rich. They now think we own that York candle company up in Alaska and York Fitness home gyms. Our lips are sealed. The town calls our street Yorkville. The rest of the extended family are also living further down our street, and we keep all the land vacant over the road at the even-numbered lots to not obscure our valley views.

Sparky was now a registered 'sparky' with his own company of the same name; all the new people arriving in our little mountain town never knew the reason behind his name; they assumed Sparky was due to his business. He is very good at solving everyone's electrical issues, no doubt. But he got himself into a pickle when he was 16. The house that was attached to the bakery, the home of Henry, our baker, had an issue to be fixed. It turned into a real big pickle when Henry's daughter, Hens, was admitted to the little local hospital with 'burns to her nether regions;' I guess

Sparky got a bit friendly with the baker's daughter for the first and last time.

"Kids will be kids," I told them, trying to smooth it over. We loved that bakery; a couple of new bakeries have opened up in town due to demand, but we still go to 'Sparky's bakery' for the best cinnamon buns ever made. Henry was the Cinnamon Bun Superstar.

Sparky did turn a few heads when the newcomers arrived. His large, tanned frame, muscular physique, and pure snow-white hair had always been like that since he was born. He wore his hair long, in a man-bun, way before man-buns were popular. I continually wanted him to chop his hair but he said no, it 'took all of his power away,' so he kept his long hair as-is. He looked like a real superhero.

He was an adventurer and a dreamer, he had lots of ideas for himself but loved the mountains. He hunted well and provided food for all the York family along Yorkville. He would go up to the cabins we owned a couple of days north of here. Only he ever went there, to the hunting cabins; he loved nature.

Sparky was also a brilliant sketch artist. He produced the most brilliant works as a young child, dabbled in oil on canvas, and even won first prize in a neighboring town's competition before he completed his apprenticeship.

I never thought the day would come.

But it did.

There was an older white-haired man about town asking about a baby that was born 22 years ago. "He may have pure-white hair," said the man. Henry raced up and told me. Not just any kind of gray hair, but *white, pure white.*

"Where is Sparky, Darlene?" said Henry.

"Up at Ridge Cabin, Hen!"

"Thank God, is he staying up there for a while?"

"Yeh, he has three weeks off work, havin' a real good break, he has been tired lately. He took the snowmobile up there."

"Ah good!" and Henry went quickly back down the hill. He turned about and I know Hens was going to get a report, I know she was secretly in love with Sparky still from when they were 16, but afraid of him for life. Hens would tell everyone about town to keep their mouths shut, as a town we all were very good at looking after our own. It's just those newcomers that have to be told, that Hens will fix it.

"Yeh, he is around here, I've seen him, Sparky's Electrical," said a new florist woman who had moved into the old Smokers Hut.

"SHIT. WHAT? Someone is living in the Smokers Hut, are you kidding me?" I said to Hens.

"Yeh, she has made it into a 'tiny home,' Darlene!"

"Get Roggie to go burn it down!" I snuffled at her, nearly coughing from the surprise of the accusation about Sparky's whereabouts and someone trying to live in a 3x3 outhouse.

"OK." Hens made it quickly down the snowy lane. Towards the fire station.

Roggie, our fire warder, was amazing at 'tying up all our loose ends.' I could see the fire from my front porch. The lady was in the neighboring town so she wasn't hurt, she would just get a nasty surprise when she got back. Town justice.

I hid Sparky's Dodge in the garage up at York's 48 property on Yorkville out of sight.

"The town is silenced," Hens told me along the town grapevine. A 'prayer-chain' was summoned for Sparky and the man left without any issue.

"We're running low on cash, Darlene," said Al the next day after the man left town. "You'll have to get Sparky to get new numbers for us when he gets back."

"OK, Al."

My husband Al was so good at looking after all the finances. Such a relief that I didn't have to do it anymore, I hated running the books.

"Mother!" called Sparky when he returned two weeks later on the snowmobile with two white-tailed deer tied on the back. "Get the smoker fired up, I've got good ones."
I had never told him that I wasn't his real mother, or what had happened all those years ago. Maybe I should have, but there was never a right time and it never seemed to come up.
"Mother, I have to tell you something," Sparky pulled me aside while the deer were smoking.
"Me too, I have to tell you something also."
But all the other Yorks of Yorkville arrived and we didn't have the conversation, it had to wait.

The day came after the Yorks' party died down.
"You know I've been going up to the cabin for a couple of years on and off?" Sparky started. "Well…you know those 'Yeti People' from the far mountain range?" He continued, and my eyes widened so much I nearly became an owl. "I have someone I want you to meet…" A tall, pure white-haired lady came walking around the corner holding a white-haired baby, and a white-haired toddler held her other hand. "This is my girlfriend, Mom, and my two kids, and the other man is my soon-to-be father-in-law," as a white-haired man followed. Sparky had found 'his people' – he was a Yeti Person from the far mountains, and he carried a full bag of cash for us too. I didn't have to tell him my secret, I guess he already knew instinctively.
"Mom, you're next!"

8. Let's Go Back to This Day.

"Look up. My eyes are up here!" I say, looking at Jeremy's astonished expression as I usher him onto my hydrangea-clad patio, coffee in hand, splashing it everywhere on the paving.

Summer – thank you for the memories. Thank you for the bikinis, thank you for the beach cocktails, and thank you for cleavage. This has been the best day of my life. I now look back on this day, and who would have known that 12 months later, nothing is the same? I trip on the same piece of exposed pipe sticking out from under the underbrush flowering parts and old wood in my courtyard, as I did last summer and the summer before that, too, and look down at the gash in my leg, a scar upon scar; no one is laughing about it with me, no one is here, there is nothing to laugh about. So I hightail it back to my restored Adirondack outdoor suite, and I sits.

Words are funny things. So are feelings, so is security, so is bliss, so is joy, and so are cats. What's really in it all? What's this life really about? Are you important on your own island with your loved ones around you, whatever that looks like for you? Do you offer love and joy to all you meet during the day? My cat certainly does. I do find all this puzzling in the sense of the word...LOVE. Only because heartbreak happened to me on what seems like a never-ending cycle. I hope I will love again. Let's go back to this day a year before.

When the dilapidated village shop and post office building came up for sale, I bought it and moved in. Overgrown and wrinkled like an ageing woman (like me) with nature from the outside finding its way inside – a 'renovator's delight', the sales ad posted. A lost kitten had wandered in the open front door past the mail slot and was spooked by its metallic thud practically as I was, and we now live here together, and my cat taught me to zen. Our kitty love-language became so infinite that I could tell everything she was thinking. She oozed 'catitude', and my friends and I started the 'Curious Cat Society'. The meetings were held at my post office home – even habits their cats have created are hilarious, relating them as some of the funniest cat stories they know. These weekly cocktail events became our social outlet, our time to decompress, share as women, and laugh at each other's cat stories and ourselves, too – so funny they can be. They can be hysterical when they're getting ready to pounce, planning a sneak attack on others in your home, crouching low to discover something for the first time, or covering you while you are trying to type, read, or get out of bed. My now-adult Abyssinian shorthair with her sleek black coat, one white paw with white pads, and a little white heart shape near her nose, all her other feet and pads black – she not only loves boxes and confined spaces and bags but delights to cram herself into large glass jars and peer out the corner of her sparkling honey-coloured eye so enlarged by the glass, like one large disembodied eye in the jar staring at me, blinking. "If I fits, I sits." I *hear* her internal dialogue – I named her 'Sits' – so many shenanigans that make me laugh and bring so much joy to my life.

It was a nice distraction and zen from my 'working world'. I love to laugh – I love comedies, follow my favourite comedians on social media, and pop in for a little laugh and a cuppa on the couch from time to time. But more fun than that is when the owner's 22-year-old son returns home too late from outings when he comes to visit from university; the squealer will also make sure the parent knows about that too.

One Friday afternoon, when the late autumn sun was setting, our Curious Cat Society – CCS – meeting was a great excuse for bubbles this afternoon. It was a long working week with a stressful crescendo at the lab, and the other CCS members voiced the same exaggerated stress levels. Mid-conversation, after one bottle of bubbles had washed down the bickies, cheese, and fresh figs, Sits dragged over a book from the library; we all could hear the *scrape ka-thunk, scrape ka-thunk,* and witnessed an ever-increasing little line of dribble that she left behind on the stained oak floors; she often saved books from the 'donation' pile or would bring me one – again dragged by mouth – that reflected my current mood. Such an emotionally switched-on being, she surprised me every time.

"'The Dalai Lama's Cat'?" said Gemma, picking up the publication as Sits dropped it at our feet. "The attention must always be on her!" we giggled, and all of our ten pairs of hands stroked her in turn, leafing through the book for Sits' message to us. Her instant reaction of her trilling as Saffy read a passage from the book. "Oh, how adorable! I didn't know you had a cat!" she exclaimed. "Why should His Holiness (The Dalai Lama) not have a cat?" Gemma trailed off with intrigue as if reading a bedtime story to us all to deviate from our heated forensic conversation. "If only one could speak, I'm sure she would have some wisdom to share." We all agreed. Sits trilled and trilled and gave Saffy a paw-high-five, jumping up on the table, taking a few moments to curl in and around our ankles; we could feel her little tail wrapping and unwrapping itself as she passed from leg to leg, and then departed to take her position on the windowsill, and fell asleep with a long exhale.

"Message received, I guess," reacted Adele. "Imagine her eavesdropping on conversations by a vast number of people that come and go; imagine if a book was written in the tone of Sits' voice – in her narrative voice." We all giggled. But, imagine?

At the time of conception, our CCS group was a convening of friends, a Friday-knock-off-and-decompress-excuse and funny-cat-stories-giggle, that unintentionally evolved into a cold-case review group.

I am a biologist employed by a forensic laboratory, Gemma is a homicide detective, Saffy – a Himalayan – a Tibetan-Burman spiritualist, Adele's title was unknown (but we all knew that she was a type of informant/investigator who posed as a writer), and Ricky was a journalist and podcaster; we were a melting pot of intrigue. A conversation arose about a cold case Ricky was delving into from the early 1980s where the killer was never found; the suspects were all eliminated in 1980 via investigation, but from the recent DNA profiling from the reopening of the case in 2002, it was back to square one. Ricky's podcast, 'What Remains', became widely listened to, and local police took her investigative prowess seriously. Secretly, my skills were called upon, as were those of others in the group, and even Sits' set of skills was valuable to the group.

Ricky's podcast 'What Remains' studies the cold cases and the decades-long ripples they have caused. She tells her story for the first time, why she became an informer, and what happened when her double life was exposed to the world of criminals, all the while secretly working as a police informer and journalist.

A week later, a news bulletin sounded from the TV – Sits was up to her tricks again, pushing buttons. "Suspect was identifiable; police informer was found dead. The man's face was splashed over the local papers and news bulletins," sounded the news announcer. I rushed in and was interested; OUR COLD CASE UPDATE made it to the news. Sits placed her paw on the red button on the remote control and silence filled the room, before she bellowed out her repetitive high-tone meowing of happiness and fulfilment.

That was also the day a guest cat arrived; Sits was so preoccupied with her new company she totally ignored our Friday CCS cocktail night. Sits and her new 'Beau' were busy 'NestFlixing' as I watched Netflix later that night. They both sat on the second-storey kitchen windowsill looking at the birds in the nest on the other side of the glass, chirping and twittering – that's the chirping of Sits and Beau, not the sleeping birds – titillated by the visual stimulation that went on for hours. Beau stayed for days at a time. The physical comedy was highlighted with Beau around – it has always been a key part of our CCS humour, so it makes sense that it's only funnier when our agile cats fall – we all couldn't help laughing at our feline duo when Beau climbed up some curtains and almost made it to the top before falling and landing with a loud thud (on his feet of course, he is a cat!). Sits put her few words of wisdom in the mix, and she sat watching the event unfold. We could all hear her speak: "Wut?!" And saw her blink and slink away in disgust. When Beau does something he isn't supposed to, the tattler Sits will meow loudly until Mummuh checks on precisely what's gone wrong. Beau was disinvited, as he left the building and didn't return for weeks.

Occasionally, Sits looks at me with dull eyes. "Awwww, not feeling well, babe?" She natters back; I pat her as she listlessly meanders across the oak to the Damascus rug fireside. Carpeting was the answer; the expensive rug took a beating as she clawed out her frustrations, and the corners of the couch were also the answer. "Chirp chirp," as she padded over for plenty of lap-pats, and then: "Purr purr." Problem solved – I do wish life's problems could be solved as easily.

We experienced unexpected snow in winter – Sits rushed out the door, froze, looked around confused, and began jumping into the air to escape the cold white substance. Plumes of powder rushed around her, tornado-style, and she flew back in the laundry door and couldn't make a last-minute turn and ended up drifting, and slamming into the wall. Of course, it's only fun; nothing was hurt but her pride, and the disgust etched on her face ended her fun day…straight to the carpet, the destruction of couch corners, then the fireside Damascus bliss.

My writing nook is idyllic and Sits basks in the last few moments of the sunshine that day on the windowsill; I place my fresh espresso coffee on a coaster next to my desktop. I type, she purrs, and the 'Take me back to that day' rag column evolves; so nice to be paid for my hobbies and that a large magazine took me on. I read as I type, I write about kitty-humour and current events from my humorous life angle. I go for a coffee refill, and in my moment of absence, Sits now has repositioned herself on my coaster, and her right paw on the delete key… "No, Sits!" I see the muscles in her right leg start to move…the paw presses down… Click!

The following summer brought our cold-case work to a crescendo and a twist in my post-office renovation journey. During that long cold winter, many decluttering events took place. Sits assisted me, and to my surprise, clearing out the 'dark end' of the kitchen, unpacking drawers, and dismantling a built-in sideboard, I found a concealed drawer. A little kitchen drawer with a hidden half-drawer tucked behind it – I crowbarred it open and found envelopes of pictures, lots of Polaroids, black and white photos from a long-gone Victorian age, and other old film slides of a cat that looked just like Sits. The same single white paw and pure white pads, the little white heart shape near her nose. "Is it you?" I looked at her. She answered with a trill followed by a chatter; she winked and slinked away when I found a well-worn cat's collar. The little ticket attached said 'Juliet'. Another photo had the image of the same black Abyssinian shorthair with her shiny sleek coat – a large amber-coloured eye and sleek black head sticking out of a large antique blue and white porcelain ceramic jar.
"JULIET?" I looked over at Sits on her windowsill, waking her from her slumber as I said the name, "OHH ARE YOU JULIET?" She answered back again with a very chatty "MRRRR!" and other chatter. How can this be? We all discussed it at that Friday's CCS, and Saffy said intuitively that Sits was definitely, in her opinion in fact is, Juliet. The group collectively tried to trick her, both calling her name and then saying her name quietly in conversation, then adding other random names…she always answered and replied to the name Juliet with a series of repetitive

meowings.

Entwined with the cold-case advancements, life became very hectic. As time went on, things were so much more important than that – we all need motives and answers, and I had the feeling we were onto something and I felt I was being stalked. Gemma felt it was related to the case, Adele and Saffy were very concerned for my safety, and Ricky wanted a police detail on me, so Adele started to escort me home.

In the DNA lab bungle from 2002, I had rectified professionally, and it was found that the murderer in fact was one of the persons of interest back in the original 1980s investigation. Every suspect was back in the frame of the cold case and under investigation, now authorities were on the hunt for one specific man, and someone was after me to silence me. Gemma and Adele walked from my car in through the back door and checked all the doors and windows, did a sweep of all three storeys of the post office, and Sits flew into action with purpose assisting them. The front door slammed, and the old deed mail slot that was still situated in the front door (I loved it and left it there for antique and authenticity purposes) swung open and its metal flap jammed itself open, as it always did whenever the door was slammed hard enough. Sits immediately hissed and leaped into action, heading to the light switch above the bureau at the front door, and turning it off. There was a shadow on the other side of the door, and we all froze. Sits slinked her way back across the sideboard bureau, weaving in and out of the crystal bowls so silently and with agility, not touching one item, past the crystal decanters and glasses; next, *the glass jar* that she sat in with her magnified eye, and finally past the espresso machine to arrive at Gemma's handgun. And there she sits. Her paw reaches into the trigger guard and trigger, and somehow the gun fires, and the bullet goes straight through the open mail slot and straight into my stalker.

Everyone has the right to sits and zen out. I decided to retire after all the commotion of the cold case and the shot stalker (who did survive), and reopened the little store as a vintage bric-a-brac shop – I called it 'Fits &

Sits Antiques'.

I used to be a hectic woman, now I sits 'cos my new life fits. Patting Sits as she purrs, I'm in my new bikini, cocktail in hand, and cleavage exposed with Jeremy's jaw dropping. "My eyes are up here," I giggle, thinking this will be the best day of my new life. Now, many years on I sits, my eternal feline 'Juliet' sits, we sits together quietly so purrr-fectly, and Let's Go Back To This Day again.

9. Don't Forget About Elizabeth.

"Life on this plane is not too high for the divine element in human nature, but such a life will be too high for human attainment; for any man who lives it will do so not as a human but in virtue of something divine in him."
– Aristotle.

A Geelong Post article, in June 1986, brought nationwide attention and notoriety to the case of a lost Victorian girl from over 120 years ago.
What happened to Elizabeth? If you heard her calling, would you help her? Mystery surrounds her fate, and sightings have been plentiful since the 1860s, even to this day.

Sightings of Elizabeth were loosely documented for the first sixty years after her disappearance in 1863, then fell silent until the 1980s when some witnesses presented evidence of grainy photographs with luminous objects, waif-like apparitions, and shimmering heat distortions. This was the decade when intrigue into mysteries, disappearances, UFO sightings, and paranormal events all gripped the nation's attention. Initially, the search for Elizabeth had been kept alive by her distraught family members and locals, especially the close-knit shipping community, because

Elizabeth was the favourite daughter of a wealthy shipping merchant.

*****

The bow of the merchant clipper ship, *Lightning*, had taken a beating since the ship had left her origin point in Liverpool, England, but on this sunny morning in June 1863, the ship still gracefully docked at Corio Bay in Geelong, in Australia. She lived up to her reputation as one of the fastest sailing ships of her time. Her grace when fully rigged was evident and her three masts were laden with the best canvas the Americans could supply. She was a prime example of why builders shied away from shaping ships' hulls into cod heads and mackerel tails.

"There stands the colony!" Elizabeth pointed with excitement. She had been imagining her dainty shoes touching the new colony's earth, and was looking forward to removing her spindly fingers from the white silken gloves of aristocracy, and feeling at home. She dreamed of it all – turkey dinners, hot cocoa in front of the fire while she snuggled up in hand-made blankets, and loving family and friends filling her big grey house on the hill, the house her father had given to her as her marital home, for herself and Edward. *I do hope I like this Edward fellow...* She had had weeks of chanting this to herself on the voyage over.

"There stands the colony!" she shouted again from the upper deck. The long pier looked frail and narrow, nothing like its Liverpool counterpart. Hordes of men were queuing to receive the goods aboard the ship. Some very well-dressed gentlemen looked out of place on the shore amongst the ratty-looking sailors. She looked beyond and a stately three-storey building stood at the crest of the hill at the end of the pier, a distant grey sentinel standing guard for the colony, and close behind it a penal gaol, next to the chimney stacks and woolsheds along the streets behind the foreshore.

A voice whispered into her ear, "Excited to be here to start your new life, ma'am?"

Elizabeth was surprised. This was the first time on the journey that the children had been spoken to, other than by their minders. The younger children and the older teenagers had all been separated on the three-month voyage purely from the standpoint of age and social status. Katherine, Elizabeth's trusted minder, never left Elizabeth's side and had assured her mother in England that there would be a safe passage and delivery to the waiting fiancé. Elizabeth was at the age where the arranged marriage was all signed off on – not that Elizabeth was worried; an adventure to a new world sounded like just what she needed to exit her mundane elite society existence. A transformation was necessary; she was intelligent and emotionally older than her sixteen years. *New house, new friends, maybe even a pet feline.*

It was Katherine's duty to meet 'him' on the dock and then accompany the new 'them' up the hill to the new marital house, stay for a few weeks, and then take the *Lightning* back home to Liverpool.

Elizabeth's excitement was soon tempered by nausea. After stepping onto the New Holland soil, she discovered that the ground seemed to be moving strangely beneath her feet, the walkway had an ebb and flow feeling to it, and the people on the pier seemed to rhythmically flow along in unison. She became instantly ill, swaying, and Katherine caught her, unfortunately now wearing the regurgitated scones of Elizabeth's last meal down her dress.

The noise of the sailors yelling made Elizabeth's head throb. She felt dizzy and held tight to Katherine's hand. "Haul the pumpkins!" essayed from gruff voices in one direction, while "Secure the barrels!" was voiced by the deckhands.

Dignified, well-dressed men approached, shouting at each other, women screamed for their children to keep up, and a little girl snatched unsuccessfully for her hand-sewn doll as it dropped into the bay. The prospectors carried their shiny tools that glinted in Elizabeth's eyes, riggers prepared their heavy equipment, and seagulls rose up over the crowd in demand for their next meal – chaos prevailed.

"Upon my honour," a voice then boomed from down the pier, over the chaos, "there was never such a thing as beautiful in nature as YOU!" He met Elizabeth and Katherine, acknowledged Katherine's hand, and then took both Elizabeth's hands in his. He looked deep into her sparkling blue sapphire eyes. Her natural long golden locks fell over her shoulders as the wind picked up. She could read a sign of welcome on his face. "Edward," she exhaled. He kissed the back of her hand. She looked at him, but couldn't find the depths of his eyes under his chiselled eyebrows and cowlick hair. He shook Katherine's hand again like she and he were passing the baton of responsibility over. *Father's orders.*

Elizabeth recalled overhearing the conversation between her brother and mother when the match was first discussed. The Liverpool Daily Post had subsequently read:

Edward is affianced to Lady Elizabeth Dennys. Wool baron Bury St. Edmonds will send his eldest daughter to New Holland's colony.

Elizabeth had lost Katherine's hand, but now Edward clung to her like she was a newly won prize. She felt his bony elbow and frowned from underneath her wide-brimmed lace bonnet, holding onto its straps as the wind blew even harder.

"What an honour you do me, m'lady, I am at your service." He continued to talk over the noise of the pier, now squeezing her hand a little too tightly and glancing back at the *Lightning*. "Quite chilly and treacherous for you, I imagine, while the food would be more like gruel than the fare you will get at our new home." He wouldn't stop talking.

Elizabeth concentrated on her rickety steps and nausea rather than on his whiny voice. She wouldn't say boo – the ship's food had been delicious and plentiful, the sailing adventure amazing. She had had lucid dreams of thrilling adventures on the high seas: the Pfalz sails flying high as she peered up towards the crow's nest from the oiled deck, witnessing the high rigger hanging on with only his legs as he saved the sail from ripping off its conifer frames – so much excitement.

Edward banged on about the pitfalls of travelling, and she zeroed his voice out. "Yes, sir, palatable," she choked out, to offer some sort of conversation piece. She thought he might stop his prattling and whistling his words through his teeth. She sighed and grimaced as she was ripped from his elbow. She was pushed by the herding crowd in the opposite direction back towards the 370-pound wool bales and the rows of sour-smelling, stinking, shackled men – wolf-whistling rudely at her as she flowed by.

As she called out for the disappearing Katherine and Edward, she watched his slicked crown fade away, and her stomach dropped as the realisation hit her of the magnitude of her predicament. She held her breath against the smell of the rotten fish even as the spilled remnants on the wooden pier made her fine polished shoes all sticky. She ducked quickly as a load of wool bales was swung too close overhead, shuddering at the near miss. She could hear the sound of the bullock wagons in the street, no doubt here to collect her father's 4,000-bale wool shipment, now in the process of being loaded onto barges to be taken ashore. Edward's voice then came from somewhere in the crowd: "ELIZABETH! ELIZABETH!"

A sudden sharp pain exploded at her right temple, and dizziness overwhelmed her. She felt her head – blood everywhere, flowing rapidly. She felt a hard knock on her shoulder and recognised the coarse hessian fibres now scratching her face as she was pinned up against the stacked wool bales. The escaping red fluid was hot on her cheek and stung her eyes; she blinked and rubbed them, and the pain in her head worsened. She heard her name being called again by Edward and now Katherine too; she could hear the panic in their voices as the pier faded away and vanished.

*****

Total silence now surrounded her.
She looked around the dock with clear eyes and no pain in her head, but no one was there.
Gone.
She squinted and tried to focus in the bright morning light, and shook her

head. No foggy haze in her vision, just no one anywhere.

"Hello?" Confused.

Everyone had truly gone.

Dead noise.

She could hear the waves, and the seagulls, see the coastline, stomp her feet; her now-pristine white shoes tip-tapped on the bare wooden pier. Not a single ship in sight, no piles of cargo, nobody anywhere.

"KATHERINE? EDWARD?" No one answered. "HELP?"

She continued to call out, walk about; she cried, she shook, she walked, she stopped, she yelled. Her nose was warm to the touch. But no stinky fish, no sour men in shackles, she didn't feel the cold, or feel the wind or the sun – but she could hear. She reached the end of the abandoned pier and could hear birds. She looked down, and now her dress was tatty as if it was now a hundred years old, and her lace bonnet was gone.

She felt for her bleeding skull with her numb fingers, but nothing. No blood, no wound, no matted hair. She closed her eyes and chanted to herself, hoping she would open her eyes and the world would be back to normal, like when she had played imagination games with her younger brother as a child. She opened her eyes; the formerly chaotic pier was still silent. No Katherine taking her to her new life, not even prattling Edward. She looked at the land with a vacant expression; the seagulls had also now fallen silent, muted as they circled above her, no sound at all – inanimate silence.

An icy chill began to develop and the surrounding environment suddenly became very cold; fog surrounded her, falling over her shoulders, collapsing around her like a blanket falling and drifting down to her feet. She held out her arms, she saw her hands, and turned them over; she looked pale and sick. Pallid, her palms were very white; she felt her face, but still no blood. She could feel water splashing her face, it was overwhelmingly salty and grainy in her mouth. Looking down at the wharf she could see little waves, then bigger waves, then movement under the pier's wooden planks spaced sparsely, all peeling and worn.

She rocked back and forth a little, standing there for what felt like an eternity, imagining herself falling into the water, maybe becoming a mermaid (like she had spoken about with Katherine over many shared adventure books, the perfect escape from any situation – imagine you are elsewhere, a happier place). Katherine had always hated that Elizabeth walked so close to edges whenever they were waterside. Katherine knew she would jump in, and swim down to invisible cavernous subterranean worlds and mythical creatures. She recalled being laughed at by a young man in Liverpool at her schooling class that Katherine had led. His skinny but capable arms had flailed around making swimming gestures, pretending to be one magical creature, using his cinnamon squirrel cap as a prop of ridicule – in fits of laughter.

"KATHERINE, WHERE ARE YOU?" Jolting back to reality, now in a panicked state, yelling. Chanting over and over as she walked briskly towards the woolsheds, she would go and find someone. Everyone can't just disappear.

Everything now looked totally different, again.

She imagined turning a corner and Katherine would be there, welcoming her to her arms, to feel safe again in her minder's embrace. SAFE. They would soon be sat in front of a crackling fire, drinking cocoa and eating scones and croissants, as they always did after a stressful day. More images filled her mind of a life with a loving family, turkey in the oven and the smells filling the house, hearing people laughing and giggling. But that didn't happen. She now sat alone in the woolshed with only large amounts of wool for company. Solo. Sitting in deafening silence…

As though in answer to her urgent prayer, a repetitive knock sounded nearby, tap-tap-tap in a rhythmical three-knock sequence. "HELLO!" Elizabeth called out, "IS SOMEONE THERE?"

Elizabeth continued to get up, sit down, and at times run around (with a snotty nose and puffy eyes) towards random noises; knocking, loud banging, chattering, glass-hitting-floor sounds, child toy rattle sounds. Nothing to see, only hear.

Hair now tatty to match her dress, gloveless hands now bony, and now bare feet falling heavily in exhaustion over shards of broken glass. *Where did my shoes go?* So confused, she shook her head, sat down – face in hands, she sobbed; tearless sobs.

"HELLO?" Elizabeth's eyes flashed open, but she was otherwise too exhausted to move. A disembodied voice chimed in from somewhere: "Hello? If anyone is there and would like to make contact, just speak and we will hear you."
"HELLO, HELLO, I'M HERE, IT'S ELIZABETH, WHERE ARE YOU?" Shouting, hoping desperately to see someone come around a corner, she continued to look around, holding her breath for silence. The noise of her own inhaling and a strange exhale wheeze was deafening. The room was dark, her eyes wide open, raindrops chased each other down a broken window near her with the repetitive drop-drop on the wooden floors not far from her feet. The dark shadow of twilight danced around the walls…there was that knock again, that same repetitive style three-sequence knock. She reached down to the floorboard and repeated the knock as if to answer. Silence.
A 'knock-knock-knock' came back. She repeated it, and then the knock answered her again in the same sequence pattern.

The space seemed to change somehow. The room seemed lighter as if an invisible fog had lifted, but silent. She stood up and walked outside; no pain issued from her now savagely sliced feet, and no blood either, no sensation at all. The sun now shone brightly, morning had breached, and she had no sense of time. Two minutes ago, the sun was fading and sunset made the fading light dance, now sunrise. As she stepped out into the sun, the sun shot up quickly in the sky to right above her head and the heat was intense on her poor-quality skin. The outside space rapidly changed, she could *feel* static energy in the air, and her hair stood on end. The young sapling she stood next to suddenly and instantly shot up into a 30-foot tree, the branches reaching high into the sky vertically, and spreading wide, and then new leaves sprouted and cast a magnificent shade over her.

Noises came and went as she span around – adults speaking, kids laughing, noises that sounded like one of those out-of-hand adult parties her father had hosted back in Liverpool. She could now feel the energy and activity of many people, she even felt the nudge of shoulders and people walking by touching her by accident, but saw no one. She could hear music and conversations word for word; people talking about television, the Ferris wheel, taking rides, Netflix, eating fairy floss.
So strange.
Nothing made any sense.
In one instance, she thought she saw someone walk by. "Hello, is anyone there?" she shouted over and over into the abandoned space around her. She thought to herself. *"Katherine?"* She realised her spoken voice had become just a voice in her head.
She had never felt more alone.

*****

Elizabeth smelled smoke. There was no evidence of a fire, but ashes fell around her; it was suddenly night, the rain fell, the sunrise was then brilliant, the wind picked up, and newspapers flew by. A sheet of paper tumbled past her feet and got caught on her shin; another then slapped her in the face. She peeled off the paper and read the strange bold writing:

> **What happened to Elizabeth? What do we know about her disappearance?**

"EEEELLLLIIIZZZAAABEEETHHHHHHH," came a wispy, faint, disembodied voice, caught in the wind. "COMMMME BAAAACK INNNSSSIIIDE," the voice entreated, as she continued to scan the newspaper page for information:

> **Elizabeth Dennys investigation reopened after 153 years, the longest cold case in Australia's history. Potential new evidence found after recent fire in the old Geelong woolsheds.**

Elizabeth felt nauseated and froze. *One hundred and fifty-three…YEARS?*

"EEEELLLLIIIZZZAAABEEETHHHHHHH," repeated the voice.

"I'M HERE, I'M HERE, WHERE ARE YOU?" she frantically waved her arms, ran around a little, and then headed back to the woolsheds after the instruction came to her once again: "COMMMME BAAAACK INNNSSSIIIDE!"

She entered the woolshed via a side door and froze. A lady now stood at the far end of the packing room – a lady wearing clothing of a style unfamiliar to Elizabeth, and with her dark hair cut much shorter than Elizabeth was used to seeing on a woman. Next to the dark-haired lady stood a man holding strange little boxes with green lights flashing. A rod was on the lady's other side, making a whirring and buzzing noise. Elizabeth was more confused than ever.

The man suddenly gasped. "The Rem-Pod!" he said, pointing at the flashing device in his hand, and then signalling to the lady.

"Hello, is that you, Elizabeth?" the lady said. "We were hoping you would be here. We'd love to connect with you, if that's okay?"

"Yes, I'm Elizabeth Dennys. What has happened? Who are you? What happened to Katherine?" Elizabeth blurted all this out in one quick breath, not sure if her words were actually spoken or the kind that were in her head. Her teeth clenched, and she stepped towards the lady. The man shook. "She's…she's coming towards you, Rach," he stammered out.

"You can use my energy if you need to," the lady continued. "Come next to me, and let's have a chat, and I can fill you in."

Use her energy? What is she talking about? So strange. Elizabeth now noticed other voices, and felt other bodies – bodies of energy – around her, some hostile, some kind, some just as confused as she was. She could then see wispy figures dancing around her in the now darkened room, passing through the door, past the window, or some just standing there, staring at nothing.

"Are you still there, Elizabeth?" the lady repeated a few times. "Can you make yourself appear to us so we can see you?"

Elizabeth stood next to the lady and could feel a cold tingling sensation.

The lady's image became very clear, and Elizabeth too felt her energy shift to a kind of clarity; her hands felt warm and supple, her hair was less tatty, and her white dress seemed a whiter shade, and now ironed.

"Hello, Elizabeth," the lady inhaled deeply, "I'm Rachel, nice to meet you. We mean no harm. This is my husband, Edward." The lady pointed at the man with the devices. He wasn't Elizabeth's Edward, but when he spoke, he did whistle through his teeth.

"YES! I'M ELIZABETH DENNYS." *How can I make them see me?* She went up to them and shouted in their faces, nose to nose. They just stared blankly as if they were blind, and they were unmoved.

"We acknowledge you, Elizabeth, we know who you are, and we want to talk about what you are," the lady called Rachel continued.

Think, think, think, Lillybet. Again, Elizabeth chanted to herself.

"Something has happened to me; I'm somehow trapped here, or stuck; no one is here with me, I was at the busy pier, and then everyone just disappeared," she chattered, not expecting them to hear her.

"We know, Elizabeth," said Rachel, "that you went missing, vanished." Noticing some pieces of loose glass on the floor, Elizabeth scooped them up and threw them, so that they landed at the lady's feet…the lady gasped and jumped back, and the man called Edward screamed. *THEY ARE AWARE OF ME!* Elizabeth's eyes opened just as wide as those of the others in the room.

"Was that you, Elizabeth, throwing glass?"

Thank the Lord. "Yes, it's me, getting your attention."

"Elizabeth, we are looking for you, we have been for years. Please use some of my energy so that we can see you come closer." The lady had her eyes closed as if she were concentrating. Elizabeth approached her again, so close that she could breathe on her neck. Rachel shivered, while Elizabeth heated up and felt static in the air, and could hear it too; her hair stood on end, and she tucked a few stray hairs behind her ears.

"Get close to me, Elizabeth, feel my energy and take some; we will be able to see you, and you can see us."

"I CANNN SEEEE YOOUUUU," an eerie breathy voice leached out of

Elizabeth's mouth, even surprising her; how tinny and echoey her voice sounded and how slow it was, as she gradually manifested into a clear apparition.

"There you are!" Rachel recoiled at Elizabeth's close proximity and the sudden icy chill in the air. A jolt hit the back of Elizabeth's neck, and shocked, she lurched forward and collided with Rachel's shoulder. Edward screamed again and Rachel squealed too, yet instinctively caught Elizabeth to her body, immediately feeling a hot, searing pain through her arms as full contact occurred and was then abruptly broken. Both women picked themselves up, and their clothing swished and shook, but no wind or breeze was present. Thoughts of pain circled in both of their minds; Elizabeth couldn't believe the contact and 'feeling' she had for the longest time, while Rachel was surprised at the connection. Next were thoughts of communication and touch, and then again confusion from Elizabeth and astonishment from Rachel. Elizabeth reached out, and as she felt the connection again as she touched Rachel, she could feel her fingers moving inside her own body, like she was moving inside a costume, or her fingers were moving inside a glove.

"Who are you, Rachel? What's happened to me?"

"Oh, Elizabeth, we can help you…"

Connection lost, total silence.

Silence.

No visions.

No connection.

No communication.

"HELLO?" Elizabeth cried, and frantically yelled. Only more silence in reply.

Elizabeth stood alone in the abandoned woolshed, with rain pelting down on the roof, wind blowing in the open doors, and broken glass everywhere.

Rachel and Edward stood in the abandoned woolshed, with rain pelting down on the roof, wind blowing in the open doors, and broken glass everywhere. "HELLO?" Rachel yelled out, trying to raise her voice louder than the rain. Silence.

After that, for a very long time, Rachel would go back weekly to the same spot. Every Sunday, trying to make contact with Elizabeth again. Nothing...

*****

With the ebb and flow of the tide, the seasons changed. A scorching summer was when the woolshed would reach over 42 degrees Celsius, winter was sleet and hail, and spring bore butterflies by the thousands one week. One year, after the historic woolshed had been semi-restored and repurposed as the headquarters for a car club, Rachel became a member of the club and purchased a 1952 Ford Crestline to ensure herself continued access to the site (so she no longer trespassed; no need for bolt cutters and secrecy). Constantly searching for Elizabeth...but still nothing. A couple of grainy photos Edward had captured *that* day renewed interest locally for a while, in those who were interested in the paranormal, or history, or both.

Elizabeth sat and sat, cried with her head in her hands, then it seemed to her that after days and nights of crying with no tears, and more days and nights later, her arms grew frail. She found herself aimlessly wandering, then standing under the tall tree outside, then feeling the people go by, then doing the same things over and over and over on repeat – constantly thinking of all that Rachel had said. *Think, think, think, Lillybet. The glass worked, the touch worked, the feeling worked.*
She had a plan.
She went back inside the woolshed and commenced…

*****

"Hello, is anyone there? Elizabeth?" Rachel began her usual Sunday afternoon routine at the woolshed. She had it down to a fine art. She had upgraded her equipment periodically over the past eight years, but the routine basically never changed.

She had driven her Crestline around the back and parked behind the office. Taken her gear into the location at which she had connected with Elizabeth. Now she held her K2 EMF detector in front of her, watching the screen, hoping to see the display light up from amber to green to red, locating an electromagnetic field in her pathway as she walked in. She dumped her things in the middle of the woolshed and unpacked her bag. Last week had been her 43rd birthday, and her new EMF pump was gifted to her by her long-time friend Ned. Rachel and Ned had formed a paranormal group ten years ago now. Rachel's husband Edward had also been a member, until he became too unwell for active participation. Edward had fallen ill soon after the initial 'Elizabeth connection', and had sadly passed away – from 'natural causes' – only a year ago.

As a result of her experiences with Ned and other paranormal investigation groups, Rachel was now well versed in the casualties of collapsed graves, lichen-covered stones, uneven pathways, and spiny cactus gouged-in shins, as she and Ned would complete investigations all over Victoria. In fact they now had their own TV show and would soon be conducting interviews with UK paranormal groups and doing some podcasts.

"Hello, Elizabeth?" The EMF pump was virtually silent, only emitting a tiny high-pitched 'bleep' noise in conjunction with the red flashing button on top that shone brightly in the inky blackness of the early evening.

It was particularly dark inside the woolshed. Rachel's eyes widened and her ears pricked…listening. Rachel rolled a large marble along the floorboards; it skipped as it kicked itself over a protruding nail. The EMF pump sounded and blinked again. The marble abruptly stopped and then was sent directly back to Rachel at a pace that bounced it up to Rachel's face when it connected again with the nail. The walls rattled, windows exploded, and chamber music blasted in from somewhere. A deafening continuous high-pitched scream rose above the music, and Rachel regretted coming alone. A hollow image of a policeman wafted in and out of the far doorway, an empty nun's habit drifted back and forth, replaying over and over, disappearing and reappearing with a disembodied chuckle. A nurse and a maid ran quickly in and out along the back of the woolshed, in and out of dark patches, as a large bundle of threads fell from the ceiling, then a gust of wind rolled the bundle along like a tumbleweed, before it rose to the ceiling in an invisible updraft, then fell again and rolled and elevated – all that too on a continuous reel.

With each movement, a different trigger device would flash and sound – what a total nightmare. Rachel froze. She felt a cool hand slip into hers. She jumped what felt like a giant leap, and the hand squeezing hers pulled her back. She recognised the squeeze – Edward!

"EDWARD?" The hand squeezed again, but she looked down to nothing but the K2 meter going crazy in her hand – red-red-red-red flashing.

"RACHEL! RACHEL!" She could hear two distinct voices, one male and one female.

"Edward? Elizabeth?" Rachel gasped, short of breath.

A spiral staircase materialised in the middle of the shed, and a female apparition gracefully descended but then disappeared before Rachel could see the face. The whistle of a train sounded far off, then the sound of the train itself came rumbling through, then quickly faded. Thunder was all around her. Then audible footsteps. Closer. Louder.

The last of the remaining glass in the woolshed windows rattled in the frames, a loose door sprang off its hinges, an iron sheet flew past, and another loose item was airborne – flying close past Rachel's right temple. A dark mass formed next to her, and a foul smell filled the space – fetid, putrid. A large black truck tyre rolled in, and pinned Rachel against the wall. Rachel felt the negative energy, the hatred, and the dangerousness.

"Elizabeth, Edward – HELP ME!" Rachel choked out desperately, just as she lost consciousness and fell to the floor.

An apparition instantly appeared beside Rachel's prone form – a girl in a long white dress and a pretty lace bonnet. The apparition pulled at Rachel's right arm.

*****

Ned had felt that something would happen with Rachel tonight. He had come down to the woolshed because he knew that Rachel would be there on the anniversary of Edward's death and the anniversary of the Elizabeth sighting – both anniversaries coincided. Ned raced in through the rain, entering via the far door, with his cigarette balanced ridiculously on his lower lip as his mouth hung wide open in shock. A black mass had now enveloped Rachel's left leg and left arm, and her body was being manipulated violently, but the ghost of Elizabeth Dennys stood her ground. The spectre girl now created a white mist vortex, which moved conically and vertically. The train sound started again, and the ghost girl and Rachel were lifted up inside the vortex, high into the air away from the dark mass now writhing on its own on the floor. Rachel's limp body was held by Elizabeth's arms as they travelled.

The image of the girl carrying Rachel disappeared as quickly as a finger-snap. A bright flash lit the room. Ned experienced an instant of a million blue eyes looking at him, then a blank. Darkness, with no noise.

"Wake up! Wake up!" Rachel kicked at Ned's boot. "You've been out for like, 20 minutes, old fella!"

Ned squinted up at her from his supine position on the woolshed floor. He had no idea why he was lying down. His head hurt. He blinked, and felt a severe pain on the side of his head. He touched where the pain was – sticky, and he could smell the blood without even looking down at his fingers.

"It's just a scratch," Rachel booted him again, "now come on!" She was clearly in a hurry, as she exited the woolshed at a run.

"What the hell happened?" he chased her down, as best he could, while alternatively cradling his head and rubbing his other arm, which also seemed to be injured. He looked at his watch. It had stopped at 11.34 pm, and now the sun was up.

"What's going on, Rach?" He was nearly choking trying to catch his breath. "You were lying there unconscious like you were dead, and the girl, she was here, saving you from the muck on the floor!" He expelled most of his breath on that last sentence.

"What are you talking about, Ned?" Rachel turned and laughed at him, with her wild blue electric eyes dancing. "You're rambling crazy stuff, bro!"

Ned pressed on his gaping head injury, certainly not just a scratch, as he began to realise he was in trouble. Rachel seemed to have emerged completely unaffected by the chaos of the night before, and in fact looked bright and rested, and far too youthful and refreshed. Ned stumbled, yet continued to follow Rachel. Dizzy, his eyebrows rose up his forehead, as he realised they were now standing on the porch of the historic grey stone Dennys mansion that stood as a sentinel just up the hill from the woolshed. Rachel put an old key in the keyhole and opened the front door. She went into the house and he was compelled to follow her.

"RACH!" Ned grabbed her hand, and she turned on her heels quickly. Blue eyes shone back at him as she flung her now instantly blonde hair around, letting it cascade down to her fine waist. "You can call me Elizabeth," she whispered, in a very low-toned and silky voice.

Ned froze.

Odours of roasting meat now wafted past them.

He watched her pad gently over the floorboards, take off her wide-brimmed bonnet, and place it on the wall rack, as if she had done this a thousand times before. She walked past some mahogany antiques to another doorway, and disappeared into a great room.

*****

Ned found himself waking up again. This time he was in an old chair in an unfamiliar room, and surrounded by many unfamiliar people. Elizabeth was bent over him, wiping his face with a cloth, before she straightened elegantly and pulled at his hand, beckoning him to stand up.

"Come on, Edward. It's our special day."

He stood, and everyone clapped. "I can't believe you passed out on our wedding day," Elizabeth said.

He felt his tender head, but nothing. His hair was slicked back, and he looked down, to see himself wearing something like a tuxedo. He caught his reflection in the mirror, and it showed a Victorian gentleman. Elizabeth came to stand next to him, and there they were – a bride and groom, staring back at him from the mirror.

He felt a jolt of panic.

He whirled around. A nurse, a maid, a nun and a policemen all stood there, clapping but otherwise silent. A roaring open fire was lit and there were candles everywhere. A frail old lady was sitting on the couch by the fire. Her head was slumped, and she wore old ratty clothing. She looked up at him with dull eyes. "RACH?" He meant it as a scream, but it came out as a squeal-whisper. His eyes darted around in confusion, hoping to find answers to his many unvoiced questions. His long-time friend just vacantly stared back, soulless.

"Sorry, Ned," said a soft voice behind him, "but I had to."

A dark-formed humanoid shadow moved slowly past behind him, nauseating him, and then Elizabeth came into clear view, standing there in an immaculate white dress and long silky white gloves. She was holding a steaming cup of cocoa; she handed it to him, and he dazedly accepted it. The other guests now sat on the couch with Rachel, knitted blankets on their knees. A voice bellowed from the kitchen, "The turkey is ready!"

"Oh, my dream has come true!" Elizabeth snapped her gloves and shot her new husband a wink and a look of satisfaction from her iridescent blue sapphire eyes. A black cat purred, and wove itself gently between their feet.

10. Confetti of Ash.

The factory roof became unrecognisable and warped into strange shapes as the intense heat scorched the metal and the smoke billowed, turning the day into night.

As I sat cradling my morning coffee in the kitchen, my Birman, Charlie, affectionately curled his tail around my ankle. The day was going to be a scorcher; I could feel it in the air already. This day it would reach over 40 degrees Celsius, and the north wind would whistle around my suburban home. My pager screeched the ear-piercing continuous BEEP with the text display alerting me to a 'grass fire now spreading'. Usually the warning issued does not require an immediate response, yet I felt compelled this day to act swiftly, running out and forgetting my socks. Boots on – sockless – now aboard the pumper with my team, as a large plume of black smoke hurled itself up over the horizon, and red embers flew in a rage all around us. The factory roof came into view, and it was clear the fire had left a trail of disaster already, more than just a fast-moving grass fire. At the station, we had raced to get our wildfire gear, and I loaded the structure gear too and as our 1,600-litre pumper powered down the narrow streets passing schools and houses, the radio message received was, "This is a go-er." Our years of volunteer rural fire training paid off that day; we were directed to a steel warehouse where the rear of the factory had morphed and become disfigured, and the towers had collapsed. The crew worked well and deployed the hoses, soon getting the factory blaze under control but the fire had spread on to the trees and stumps, and our application made little difference. The wildfire had travelled down the train lines and then jumped the tracks where many residents and onlookers had been gathering earlier. The pace of the fire was astonishing. The enormity of the situation soon become very clear and evacuation time was nil. We carried out our list of instructions as the support crew to larger crews. An elderly man stood in a flannel shirt and was getting his garden hose out as the sky turned pink, then to red, then a veil of blackness descended. The fire raged and was chewing through anything in its path, even the flannelled man; there was little we could do. Ash confetti rained down, the woodyard was next, then alight and fuelled the blaze, and it raced down to the park back closer to my home. Our crew was redirected to assist with asset-protection duties. The journey was littered with police vehicles, control points, civilian cars blackened and burnt out; as we got closer it looked like an Armageddon scene. The advancing fireline was approaching from three directions – flames starting to climb up our rig's windows. It was surreal to witness trees ablaze, flames morphing into eerie shapes and angry curls; a lone tree had collapsed and a fire crew were hastily chainsawing it into pieces so we could all get through. This was not a good situation to be in.

Our driver made evasive actions as a eucalyptus tree smashed at our pumper, the smell of the volatile oils detectable from behind our breathing apparatus. "MAYDAY, MAYDAY!" The call was received as we arrived at our destination. A local crew was in severe danger on the incoming band. "Hastings Pumper on, over," came the call. "Hastings Pumper, go ahead!" "Please report to the Mayday call from Central." "Roger," we replied, and off we were in response. Large numbers of TV crews were in attendance along the way and the general public were clearly ignoring the announcements and emergency vehicles – a safe distance was not achievable in this space and visibility was rapidly deteriorating. I could feel the heat quickly coming in now through the thick glass as we continued towards the crew in distress. We located the crew that had issued the Mayday call. We collected them and abandoned their vehicle, and continued back to the local 'safer' area, dropped them off and were redeployed to a residential area under imminent threat. Residents were leaving for help as we approached. When disembarking our pumper the intensity of the winds nearly had us off our feet; the only way to stay upright was to lean into the wind. The heat was trying to penetrate our protective gear; the hot radiating sensation was like facing the Devil himself. I recall thoughts of saving homes, thoughts rushed into my head of my own home and how it was faring, but this was not a time to think of myself. Sixty homes were lost that day, and 120 more were under threat. Reports were coming in of impending losses and active crews, and everyone was doing their best to save property, goods, livestock and pets. The threatened areas consisted of gorgeous new builds, perfectly landscaped yards, sweeping views of the valley, symmetrically lined streets with brick construction and weeping cherry trees, vintage climbing roses and azaleas in full bloom – with an advancing fire front. Spot fires stared to dot around us, embers flew at our faces, dense smoke, and then the fire was there in front of us. It looked like nests of slithering fiery snakes were all around us – serpents of fire hissing and lunging at everything, and the manicured gardens were now blackened in an instant. I held the hose and approached the house, as a kitty darted past me to safety and I caught a glimpse of the large TV inside the home showing a news report of the devastation and the vast fire front – surreal. The deck was on fire, the garage was engulfed and the surrounding trees harboured gusty fireballs glowing in the darkness and threatening to take off.

The heat was unbearable and the order to retreat was given. Heading to the safety of the pumper, a fireball flew past my head and I looked down to see only my torso, while my feet and legs were shrouded in smoke and fire and the world was glowing around me. Air assistance arrived and we were drenched in water as we jumped into the pumper. We had become the subject of a Mayday call ourselves as the wind changed and the fire front moved inbound and engulfed our position in less than a minute. The air assistance was now directly overhead. The winds slowed but the downward rotors encouraged flying debris over our crew and pumper – all personnel made it back to safety and we huddled inside as instructed. The helicopter's sound is now embedded in my subconscious for life. Back on the street a chaotic scene prevailed. Ambulances were numerous, ground assistance arrived for the heat-stressed firefighters and civilians, helicopters continued to fly overhead and an Elvis Air-Crane arrived also. Animals were fleeing, kangaroos jumping past hightailing it out; numerous other tankers and pumpers arrived, carefully making their way through the debris field. There were over 300 firefighters on the ground that day.

After the debrief at the station, a meal and a rest were well received. Black fluid came out of me for days afterwards, and my nasal cavity was full of it too. A return to the site the following day healed the emotions, the mind and put my fears at rest. Residents and the public and my own wounds were collectively healing via the sense of community. I was pleased to see a very happy owner and kitty – unharmed. "Thank you for saving my home, nearly at the expense of your own," said the man.

That day 130 hectares were lost, 60 homes, wildlife no doubt but only one human life was lost (the flannelled man), thanks to the efforts of our emergency crews. Ode to them all, worldwide.

WILDCARD: Collection of 2-Minute Tales.

'DEATH CARD', BY WILDCARD

Phil Andrade. Song lyrics printed with permission from YouTube music video featuring Justin Cohen and produced by Thndrthf. January 3, 2024. Link to YouTube music video in **Connections** section.
(Expletives have been replaced with asterisked initials.)

Yeah, hey-yo, I think about death a lot, when will I go
I want to make the best of life before the end of my show
Cuz I have been so close to dying but I won't let my flow
Stop spittin' gold out my mouth like a pimp who got cold-cocked
Had Cotard delusion where I thought I was already dead
From psychotic features all up in my schizophrenic head
Had psychotic episodes my mental got dark
Felt like I died with every episode like Kenny from 'South Park'
Soul was full of sadness when I felt I don't exist
And there's just levels to the layers of the darkest loneliness
Men and women dyin' in the cold from drugs and homelessness

Then they took my close friend, now with God I've got a bone to pick
Blood in blood out, I'm crushing all your bones with picks
And my gun is like behind the scenes, cuz it has bonus clips
Life's about choices
Just like a pretty woman who gets offered lots of *D*
And she doesn't know which bone to pick, bone to pick.
This life's worth living because I'm still alive
I'm trying to find my way in it; it's hard to survive
And I know
That if it's time I should just close my eyes
In search of better days with no more hate in their eyes.
Simple said this beat was haunted and when he sent it to me
I'll be haunting all my beats with all my spirit when it's looming
And remember memories about my life and how it was
Dad said to me the meaning of this life is just to love
That *S* stuck with me forever I was reaching for hope
And Paps would be so *F* happy I'm not reaching for dope
I wonder if we get more tired as we get up in age
Cuz God's preparing us to die at the end of our days
I always want to put out music just as much as I can before I die
I'm in a rush in case I fall off again
I keep on trying real hard but my mind is housing torture
And they always think I'll fall off like the state of California
I wanted just to die, life's a painful assault
I ran in crazy situations, want to make it someone else's fault
Basically so suicidal pain is robbing you
L.A. County dudes will strangle you until your skin turns Dodger blue.
This life's worth living because I'm still alive
I'm trying to find my way in it; it's hard to survive
And I know
That if it's time I should just close my eyes
In search of better days with no more hate in their eyes.
Just know when I finally die I hope my lyrics get played

I wanted to make you laugh and help you escape all your pain
I've lived a crazy life at times, and it came equipped with lessons
My homegirl got me a bulletproof vest as a Christmas present
My friend Kim ended up inside the way of some harm
Then she died and I put her *F* name on my arm
No matter how *F* tough you are
When you love somebody and then they're just gone forever
That *S* changes your heart
God had came to me and said I got a lot to just learn
I see Kim's sister searching for a spot for her urn
And if those people really killed her then I hope you change your life
Cuz if you don't I hope you die from a hot shot and it burns
If I die before my people, baby know that I tried real hard
To be so *F* better in this crazy *A* life
Yo, but when I was alive you *M* could find me somewhere
Between the ten freeway going up to the 90
Western Promises.

***

"Oh you hate your job? Oh my God! Why didn't you say so? You know there's a support group for that, it's called everybody, they meet at the bar!" – Drew Carey.

***

DRINKING NAKED

I have always loved a little unpredictable humour. I have never seen myself as a funny person but according to my personality profile, I'm considered 'witty', my friends say this about me too, I just don't see it, my blind spot I guess.

I recently became an 'Angel' of Naked Wines Australia, I had received a $50 voucher and thought I'd love $50 of bubbles at no cost to me. Perfect. I got an email from the Naked Wines warehouse crew that my box of bubbles was on its way to my work address, Allied Health Clinic. Double perfect! "Welcome, you are one of our newest Naked Angels, we are thrilled to have you!" along with a list of member benefits. Triple perfect! My colleague announced as I walked out of my clinical room that a box was delivered for me. 'Drink Naked' in bold typeface the box read as it stood on the reception desk. "Oh, my bubbles!" I was excited. I then noticed the irony of wine delivery to a health clinic, and we all had a giggle. "I guess we are drinking Naked tonight!" which is the exact line I told my husband in a quick phone conversation in between clients. He seemed to be excited too.

I arrived home and walked in the door, and there was my husband holding two empty wine glasses, NAKED. My eyes flashed open with surprise, as did the eyes of my neighbour who stood behind me; my husband's eyes also widened, and his face flushed when he saw the bold lettering on my box of bubbles: NAKED WINES. I guess he didn't get the memo. Also, 'witty' is not what he called me. My new pet name for him is my Naked Angel.

***

"I love deadlines. I like the whooshing sound they make as they fly by." – Douglas Adams.

***

THE MONEY-TREE

When I first started writing my **SPRUIK IT!** book, I would have my Dalmatian dogs Harry and Spice under my desk, patting them with my foot and listening to them snore. I would finish a chapter, yes with them included in it, and then take them for a walk on our beach. Now, they both rest on my desk in their ornate urns with a copy of that book next to them – it was a special time in my life. Cherish each moment you have, and when it's time, cherish each wonderful memory too. When you are doing what you are doing, it doesn't seem special at all. Years later you realise it was one of the best times of your life – funny that we don't know it at the time.

"Ask and thy shall receive," my father repeated over and over when I was young. "What have you asked for?" my parents would ask me towards the end of the year, many moons ago. The day that I said, "I have asked for a Money-Tree, Dad!" his eyes flew wide open. "Ahhhh!" he replied. "Yes, that IS a good one." Mother and Father never doubted my imagination… One Christmas morning a couple of years later I awoke to our family bonsai tree, named 'I AM', a Norfolk pine that was at least 15 years my senior, sitting in the middle of the dining room table, and adorned with hundred-dollar notes. "MY MONEY-TREE!" I shouted. Never give up on your dreams, no matter how ridiculous they sound, or how many hurdles get in the way.

***

"The road to success is always under construction." – Lily Tomlin.

***

<u>POLISHED PATIENCE</u>

I've not been well versed in concealing my impatience. From a young age, I would hear my mother comfortable in the French language from her global travels – she would be calling to me in my times of agitation, "Avec de patience," and I recall when I started school the teacher said to Mother, *It's wonderful you all speak French at home*. As the famous Queen song states, "I want it all, and I want it now!" I guess this has been the theme of my life, until now. At times I can be extraordinarily patient as long as I get my way in the end.

What goes hand-in-hand with impatience? Frustration and overwhelm, well they have for me over the past 30 years. This year in 2022 I've decided to work on my patience; it seems patience testing is around each corner. I've been writing a book for too many more years than I'd like to admit. This alone is frustrating me as I write books and authorship pieces for paying clients with no trouble, but not as my personal project. I've had tech issues and lost my book three times, and recommenced over and over; luckily I have a very good memory. Lesson learned. That's only the start of my troubles regarding my book, I even convinced myself that *maybe it wasn't something I was supposed to write at all.* No! Yes, it is! *Keep going at it, Dee. But it was supposed to be completed and released in 2020. KEEP GOING.* The mental battle within myself has been horrendous, my 'pre-sales' clients have been asking, and my 'reformatting' of the book, struggles with file sizes, choices of PDF and JPG and PNG formats, have all nearly led me to destruction. PATIENCE. Daily I listen to Abraham Hicks, and to Wayne Dyer, and I consult my own cards and intuition. The recurring *themes* in 2022 for me have been 'enjoy the journey', 'there is much to learn', and 'patience is a skill developed from impatience with courage'. This led me to a conversation with a dear friend and client, this past week. "'Polished Patience'," she said.

THAT'S IT.

Polished, sparkling knowledge learned, valuable skills attained along the journey, enjoy the last few minutes as it will soon be over and on to the next adventure. POLISHED, with glamour and vibrancy.

Yesterday my book goal was completed. I polished it off, and off to the publisher it went.

I've had my patience tested, it's still negative. A journey for myself to learn from, no doubt. Time to idle my motor while I attempt to strip the gears. I know the universe is full of magical things, patiently waiting for my wits to grow sharper.

***

"The first rule of the game, is you need to play the game." – Ram Dass.

***

THE KNEE REPLACEMENT

Stuck in a room with the list of everything that annoys me: ticking clock, dripping tap, horror-movie-style creaking bathroom door hinge, roommates' freight-train snoring, and the dementia patient bed neighbour opening and closing drawers and rummaging – continuously.

I can't escape, I'm in a hospital bed and need to press the button for a nurse every time I want to move.

"We go to bed with the chooks." Sundown happens, then 7.00 pm till the wee hours are the worst.

The only thing missing from my list of 'things that annoy me in life' is the bouncing of a basketball, which funnily enough is the only thing I can think about while I'm lying here.

Tick tick, drip drip, creak creak, snore snore, rummage rummage, bounce bounce.

Drug-affected dreams would eventually plague me, with disembodied pallid fingers grabbing my half-numb legs from under the bed, and ghosts of the recently deceased visiting me during the night, wafting over me. Then after waking in fright, further sleep eludes me and it doesn't help that the dementia 'wanderers' are trying to hop into my bed at midnight. Sleep. Sleep does not come easily.

Some nights it sounds like a cocktail party happening in the hallway, with repeated conversations, arguments and many accents telling stories of far-off homelands.

For a person who lies in a recovery bed all day there actually isn't a lot of free time – it's a punishing schedule at the Valley Hospital. Nurses on pill schedules, OBS, breakfast, physio, morning 'smoko' handmade treats that I can't pick up for the cannulas and wires jutting from the back of my hands and the alarms that will sound if I move them too much. Not to mention toilet-time shenanigans, lunch, afternoon coffee, physio gym, dinner at 5.00 pm, more OBS, more pills, a shower by a different set of nurses, 'put to bed with the chooks' again (as my farmer bed neighbour expresses at sunset), and listening to the freight-trains arrive at 7.00 pm. The day is done.

There is however a nap time mid-morning and mid-afternoon if you are lucky, and sneaky snacks appear from my handbag – the stash is replenished by my amazing husband and random visitors. Powdered coffee never tasted so good after a week of nothing.

Repeat.

The set of familiar questions whizzing around the room, now after lights-out, also fly around in my own head and ricochet off my brain cells. "I'm not hungry, are you? Must be all the pills." "What's your name?" "What address is this?" "Is there a toilet here?" "Can't seem to find my things, I don't have anything here." "Gee, it's hot, are you hot?"

Repeat.

The rehabilitation gym is a welcome sight and a great hangout zone – a great alternative to the hospital bed. A 48-year-old hanging out with 80-year-olds isn't really a problem for me. The conversations revolve around, "What happened to you?" And I'm grateful for my varied knowledge set that enables me to talk to most people about the things THEY like to do. I'm popular here. Back when I first arrived via gurney for admission, I made a delightful sight for the admitting nurses, who exclaimed, "Oh, we have a young one!"

Tick tick.

Drip drip.

Creak creak.

Whistling ducks tap tap on the window at my bed and curlews creep past looking at themselves in the reflection; a welcome sight but yet another repeated sound to etch into my brain.

Tick tick. Drip drip. Creak creak. Tap tap.

Yesterday I got to sit in the sun. Blissful. I watched ants climb across my feet without feeling them tickle; I did feel the breeze pick up around my arms, and the tip of my nose got hot quickly. Sensations I hadn't realised in my busy life, now I savour the moment. That day, I AWOKE.

Now I sit on my own balcony with a freshly brewed coffee, away from all the annoying noise, and feel ALIVE – listening to the breeze, the cars in the far-off street, the rain; I feel the sun on my skin, and I love every minute of it.

***

***

MONSTER MANSION

I am 15 years into a 127-year sentence and I sit at the top of the food chain of The Lifers. A red ladybug has flown onto my knee and I watch her walk and stumble over my leg hair towards my shin as I sit in the outside cage. I get a few minutes a day in here – rain, hail, snow or shine. The other day – or was it the other week, I can't recall – an orange butterfly did a similar thing; maybe it's my mother trying to connect with me.

I was transferred to HMP Wakefield and put into solitary, and for good reason; I have no regard for human life and I admit that. Each day in the yard and hallways it's a ticking time-bomb. Who is going to die today – my fellow inmates, or will it be me? Who knows, but each day I spend my day in my own head. I do read and I look forward to that, I eat, I stretch my body, and I think. People want to know what I'm thinking about, inside the mind of a killer – a monster, sociopath, psychopath, murderer; the worst of the worst. I think of my mother, I relive my childhood each day of my life as if I live in an alternate universe of my younger self. I had a great childhood; loving, well cared-for, well-schooled…I just ended up with no respect for anyone or anything. With no remorse, I will end the existence of anyone or anything that gets in my way, or looks at me sideways. I look forward to these insects in my outdoor cage, I look forward to seeing the rat I reserve some food for each day, I look forward to drinking the milk I know is tainted with sedatives. I think about atoms, and electrons, and building treehouses, and the veins in leaves. I think about how I secretly sharpen the toilet brush's plastic handle to a sharp tip. I think about the end – the end of the next 127 years

– and I wonder how far away that will be? The ladybug's little feet tickle my leg, and she walks without wavering for anything. She spreads her mini-wings and shows me how easy it is to just fly to freedom – if only I had her skills.

***

"Life moves pretty fast. If you don't stop and look around once in a while, you could miss it." – Ferris Bueller's Day Off (1986).

***

<u>PELÉ PARK</u>

The two children had climbed the wall and dropped into the park unnoticed. The evening air was humid with the midsummer scent of jasmine flowers and the streetlamps had just kicked on. No one saw it coming, not even me at the time. Looking back on that day in my mind's movie-reel it's just so lucky that my reflexes are of football royalty's skills. I had always wanted a park named after me, and no I'm not the soccer star, but now my local park has been renamed after me, following *that* day. I reach down and my finger traces the individual letters P-E-L-É-P-A-R-K.

The two wall-climbing children were hidden from the families using the park by the long shadow cast by the light poles. I did hear, and instantly recognise, the 'click' of the butane torch lighter, followed by the 'whoosh-burner' sound. I also recognised the sound of the 'poof' of the firecracker explosion. I span around and pushed some of the other children around me away as I was seeing a fireball inbound at head height. I also recognised the ball, knowing it was a 'Flying Boy Ball Jumbo Salute Rocket' (the last time I had set one of those off was as a rebellious and unruly teen, and the magnitude of the hole it had created in the sand was immense), so the impending explosion would invariably be massive and sound like a gunshot; if the fireball landed in the crowd it would no doubt be fatal to many.

I instinctively launched myself into the air (not realising this was such a critical time in my life). "Practice, and everything else will come," was the advice my father had given to me so many years ago, the same thing that Pelé (Edson Arantes do Nascimento) was told as a child. My body soon became horizontal in the air, and I now remember it all in slow motion only – my left leg dipped, my right leg elevated, I tipped my head back to focus with the upside-down vantage point on the inbound fireball firework, and my right foot connected with it as my head was nearly at ground level. My leg then extended, and BAM, my well-practised magical style of play collided with the fireball and sent it on a trajectory headed now back in the direction from which it had come, to a far-off tree line. The firecracker in flight, rotating around its centre of gravity, seemed to have no flight drag resisting the cracker of an impact from my Pelé signature move. The fireball approached the trees at such a velocity that when it exploded in its now far-off space, leaf debris fell like confetti. The other parents and kids were all mentally computing the event and the seriousness of the matter – the firecracker's massive explosion – as the blast's soundwave intensity power-hit our ears; even from the far point of the explosion the sound force blew out some eardrums, but there was not the massacre that had been intended for so many.

The news blurb read:

> **Brave innocent bystander performs a Pelé move to save numerous parkgoers late yesterday afternoon. The park will be renamed in tribute to the hero father, who wants to remain anonymous, but who wants people to know to 'practice, and everything else will come' at the right time. He knew that learned skills could benefit many, in many ways, many times.**

***

"A little nonsense now and then is relished by the wisest men." – Willy Wonka & the Chocolate Factory (1971).

***

<u>3,000 PEOPLE</u>

When I woke up this morning I never thought I would be standing amongst 3,000 naked people in the afternoon.

I know that I have a healthy glow (courtesy of my newly spray-tanned golden skin), womanly curves, and a girlish face that brims with mischief, but at this moment, I also had the wide eyes of an owl, a jaw dropped in disbelief and shock, and surprise written on my expression. I would have choked on my own saliva if I could close my mouth. The call had come through just after breakfast. "Hi Amy, I know it's Saturday but my photographer has cancelled on me due to an emergency, and now I have an emergency of my own!" voiced my BFF, without taking a breath. "A client of mine, Spencer, needs an 'extra' – can you come, PLEASE? Filming just down from you at the Story Bridge, and bring your Canon, drybag, tripod and memory cards. See you at 4.00 pm, thanks Amy, I owe you one." CLICK went the phone line.

I guess my reply wasn't needed.

As I made my way along The Rocks, a sign read CLOSED FOR THE DAY, and I could see a wave of people along the cantilever expanse. I struggled on foot the rest of the way to the first steel truss, and there they all were...all NAKED. My face was soon to be wearing more than a healthy glow now, for the rest of the day and into the night...

'Melt Open' – live nude figures in situ, baring all for art.

***

"Why, sometimes I've believed six impossible things before breakfast."
– Alice in Wonderland (1951).

***

<u>THIS IS GOING TO END BADLY</u>

The one in the front looks like the brains of the operation and the one at the back – pay attention to all that you are weaving in your life. Transcend the challenge. I should have told her the night before, when I came home smelling of wine, or that morning, early, as I fought a thick head. But I didn't. If I had, things may be different now.

THIS IS NOT THE END. There is a little voice in my head that says, I'M DONE. This voice is combative with the other voice that says, I CAN DO THIS. Everyone's an expert at something – I am an expert at thinking everything will end in an apocalyptic event. My weekly psychologist says my catastrophising is associated with depression as well as an anxiety disorder; I know that's not me though. "This is going to end badly for me." I might need some space to try and figure things out. I was told to invent my own PARALLEL EVOLUTION. Toxic overload of chemicals, alcohol and information.

I heard her steps making their way through the lounge to me. I had learned that 'no comments' meant bad things – of course bad things – I was always expecting the worst. There was a brief pause as I finished my second coffee and I sat up stiffly, waiting for the stare, but it never came. My original plan was to start to look after my health, but I get carried away and just can't help myself. I feel (at the time) the need for instant gratification and that I DESERVE to let my hair down.

Grandmother's face curled around, wrinkled and weather-beaten from countless days spent under the sail of the harsh sun. But she came in quite happily and not disappointed in me. "I think you have come to the wrong conclusions," she said, sort of bouncing on the spot. Out of the corner of my eye, parallel to me, I saw movement and heard clanging outside. The room remained silent, as Grandmother handed me some papers. Oh, that feeling of 'it's going to end badly' flooded into every cell of my body, and I think that every pore on my skin sprang a leak. "I appreciate your support," Grandmother then said. "I used to think for many years I wasn't worth much, I wasn't ever going to have a happy existence, a happy home and a long life."

I looked up at her, puzzled. If you asked, no one could quite remember when Grandmother and Grandfather arrived in Haws Cove. After nearly fifty years it seemed as though the Cove itself became the essence of them. My mother grew up in this house, Grandfather died in this house, and I live in this house too, caring for Grandmother (but I think she cares more for me). Whether driving down to the boat launch or the main street where the older folks all sit drinking their pots of coffee all day talking about the tide, Grandmother always said, "Don't let the history of this place distract you." What did she mean? I didn't know at the time, but today I was going to find out.

My parallel evolution was unfolding, and I hadn't realised fully until I read the papers in my hand. A great technique and application, but I know I cannot get distracted from my unfolding career in the City. I had studied so long and put in so many hours establishing my credibility in my company; I cannot let history distract me.

"This is not going to end badly for you," read the first line. I turned the papers back over to the index – what was this all about? I could now see that several suit-cladded gentlemen had appeared and were standing in the hallway just off the kitchen. I hoped these papers weren't a subpoena; were the men process servers? Was it a probate? But it was a Torrens title, in fact a bunch of them. I scanned over them with my eyes and then lifted those eyes with a question to Grandmother: "Freeholds, Gram?" She returned a broad smile. "Yes, we have adapted well, Angel, we have created that *parallel* you speak of."

I still looked at her in confusion. There was a title to the local store, most of the land in the Cove, eleven properties that were tenanted, the weather station, and this house too. "We now own most of the town, Gram?"

She jumped her little skip on the spot. "These years of 'bad endings' are over, Angel. Yes, we own the town, the Cove! Although my grandfather had done many things, many kinds of jobs and was a very handy man, he was best remembered for being the milkman."

***

"You want out of the hole? First, you gotta put down the shovel." –
Incredibles 2 (2018).

***

<u>BORN TO EXIST</u>

"Toby, just ignore the bait that is dragging you down to the lower vibrations." Toby Worth leaned back in his ergonomically correct desk chair and shot a wad of paper at the box in the corner that used to hold the reams of paper. The over-the-shoulder hook shot was as dismal as his attitude as he continued to listen to the voicemail from his sister. His office neighbour, Priscilla-the-Killer, was shouting in her usual cringeworthy high-pitched tone, and the realisation hit Toby – his investment in himself of being the feature writer was never happening. He was a heck of a lot better at sailing than anything else. "You can withdraw more and more until you don't know what you want, and now you're afraid to 'want' anything. Toby, you've not laughed in years," his sister concluded, as her voice message ended abruptly.

Toby looked gloomily at his reflection in the glass wall that was the barricade between himself and Priscilla-the-Killer. *"You don't trust anyone else to have positive thoughts about you, as you don't have positive thoughts about yourself. The biggest effort you can give is another day at what you do! You weren't born to just exist, you were born to thrive. What does your own personal success mean to you?"* Toby asked his reflection. *"In business, and in life, it had been my intention to run such a tight ship... AAAND now 'Toby's successful ship' is on fire, and sinking!"*

"Well, maybe you were born to exist on the bottom of the ocean," his reflection answered him back.

***

"A laugh can be a very powerful thing. Why, sometimes in life, it's the only weapon we have." – Who Framed Roger Rabbit (1988).

***

<u>PUSSYFOOTING</u>

It's not fun to just be a participant within your reality and experience by default. It's not. It's also not fun to observe and just cope, what's fun is to hold yourself in steady alignment of what you really want out of your life, to create and grow. You can be a deliberate creator!

Visiting Cape Hillsborough's beaches, the Old Station Teahouse and picking fresh mangoes and dragon fruit with my gorgeous mother (affectionately called 'Ree-Ree') – such abundant and happy memories. We still frequent these local sites just down the road from our beach house but with Mum stuck in Victoria, we regret her absence.

Another fond memory with Mum is her saying when I was a child, "Darling, you can do, or be, anything you wish to be in this life," and I believed her. I continued to believe her up until my late twenties. Then I started to listen to others saying that I couldn't, and shouldn't, be doing things, and when I felt that my goals and dreams were a far-off fantasy, sometimes I believed all of those people. What happened to me? Were my 'pie in the sky' ambitions just that? Fast-forward to only a few years ago when my life changed due to some medical issues, and in my late forties I found solace in the words of a man about whom I had recently watched a documentary. He stated (but not in such exact pleasantries!), "When everything is messed up it's only messed up 45%, there is another 55% to work with." I LOVE THIS! I'm now 50 and I feel I have ticked each box I have ever wanted.

Let's keep our dreams and goals large, no playing small, and keep searching and working on the 55% to then attain them. Keep going, guys, and stop pussyfooting around what you REALLY want out of life.

***

"Today is a good day to try." – The Hunchback of Notre Dame (1996).

***

THE WALK

Alexa, don't skip to Friday! When you don't feel like walking your dog, remember it's their favourite part of the day, their life is shorter than yours, enjoy each moment.

***

"Generally, by the time you are Real, most of your hair has been loved off, your eyes drop out, and you get loose joints, and very shabby. But these things don't matter at all, because once you are Real, you can't be ugly, except to people who don't understand." – The Velveteen Rabbit, by Margery Williams (1922).

***

IT'S NEVER THE END

I'm so excited! And I just can't hide it! I'm about to lose control and I think I like it!

I'm channelling The Pointer Sisters' energy today. Why, you might ask? I moved our wedding date forward two months, and changed the location to the hospital courtyard so that my father could be involved. He couldn't walk me down the aisle, so I had him wheeled beside me in his hospital bed. His cancer was giving him but a few days to live, and hand-in-hand we advanced to my husband-to-be – all of us in tears, of course. Many hugs and embraces, smiles and joy…

Rachel's father passed later that night.

The joy of being newlyweds was still there, but grief-stricken Rachel sat with a half-completed manuscript over the next week. What she read one afternoon changed her life at that moment. "Another stormy day. It seems the storms of life and the stormy weather go hand-in-hand. Rainbows shine after the storm has passed, but other storms will come eventually, and you must weather them one at a time. My garden flowers live up to the challenge, and so can you. Love flips things – I go and pick up a discarded antique dressing table, sand it back, restore it and watch it in its new glorious state, to be used afresh with joy."

Rachel's eyes welled, just as much as they were to well up again that night as she was sitting in the bathroom holding the pregnancy test that would be showing a solid pink plus sign.

***

"You're trying to eat grass that isn't there. Why don't you give it a chance to grow?" – Watership Down, by Richard Adams (1972).

***

NETFLIXING

I can't even watch the last episode of a series I love, the intense desire to do so battling with my mind, knowing that when I do watch it, it's all over! I don't want it to be over, I want it to go on and on. Friends who know I watch the series all discuss characters like they are family, and events like it was happening inside their lives, and then ultimately discuss the sadness of the series coming to an end – and talk of the crescendoing details of the final episode, no doubt – and all the while I place my hands over my ears: "NONONONONO!" I can't take it. I would love a series that had the fifth of the six episodes, and just never finish it, I would rather my mind jump to conclusions than the inevitable happening. My friends call me mad! "Imagine if the stories were never completed?" they all laughed. So, then it happened. A writer friend had written a never-ending story. That's it! Like those choose-your-own adventures from my childhood. A story that will never be over. Bliss – clearly will never make it to Netflix.

***

"In an old house in Paris that was covered with vines. Lived twelve little girls in two straight lines. […] They left the house at half past nine in two straight lines in rain or shine – the smallest one was Madeline." A kind home and methodical routine is the answer to secret sauce to 'no matter what' home is home, and life is life. –
Madeline, by Ludwig Bemelmans (1939).

***

<u>BRUZA</u>

A wise mentor of ours once told me to treat your thoughts, ideas, goals, your spreadsheets and cash-flow forecasts similarly: nourish them, pay constant attention to them, feed them, love them, don't dispel them, don't ignore them, don't ever abandon them. Do them for a week, do them for a month, and never give up totally! Then tell others, and stop yourself entirely. Even before all of that though, what do you do? So many good ideas turn out to be bad ideas that often overwhelm into your life, I know I've had SO many myself! Non-productive ideas slip in, and 'hurtful ideas' are everywhere; how do you sift through them, and which ones serve you well? How do you know this at the invention of the basic idea? Life is full of storms – ARGHHH – and overwhelm, and mental confusion, and a stuff-it attitude develops even in the most positive of people, and then the 'don't do anything at all' theory arrives too. Sound familiar? I surveyed 30 people, then another 30 over time, and 98% said they abandoned their new ideas and practices within a few days and never found out if they actually served them well or not. This is how we remain stuck. Interesting that most people are stuck in something that doesn't serve them.

I am not one of them, not anymore. I was listening to one of my daily clips on a Reel about 12 months ago, and I have never been the same since. The concept is that your 'to-do list' or 'ideas' all get brain-dumped and charted on a Sunday. So I found an old diary of my own and sat down for a good read – let's revisit all that I was doing two years ago. Sorting through the list, I then categorised them ALL in a square with #1 quadrant as 2022 Goal, #2 quadrant as 2022 Goal, #3 quadrant as 2022 Goal, and #4 quadrant as Vacuum Square. Anything that ends up in the Vacuum Square GETS ELIMINATED as a 'non-serving' idea.

For example, for ME:-

- **#1 2022 Goal.** This is a lifestyle goal, facilitating a new home and marriage quality. Everything on my list for the following week that has to do with facilitating the purchase and moving to our new home and dedication to my marriage and husband, and personal and mental health, goes in this box.

- **#2 2022 Goal.** Income – passive and active revenue to a $ figure (that I do not wish to disclose here). Everything that is active income, passive income, or associated with building and leveraging $ is in this box.

- **#3 2022 Goal.** The writing and release of three (3) authorship books. Everything associated with writing, research, publishing, etc., goes in this box.

- **#4 Vacuum Square.** Every action, activity, problem, and time-consuming entry in this VACUUM box is a bad idea for me, one I then say NO to and eliminate from my coming week.

QUESTIONS:-

- Cleaning out the office and getting rid of clutter when I'm supposed to be working – is this a good idea? Yes, IN A BREAK it is a great thing to do as it supports the #1 Goal.

- Doing Tai Chi weekly in addition to my regular workout, as a bestie and I did last week, sounds like a fab idea. I enjoyed it so much – good idea? Yes, this also supports the #1 Goal.

- Adding another crypto activity to my morning routine, a good idea? Yes, supports my #2 Goal.

- Can I run an art class each month as a stand-in session, not confirmed? Can I do a talk on a podcast I'm not currently involved with, for free? Can I run another workshop extra per month? NO, so they fit into the Vacuum Square.
- Can I run a marketing campaign for someone else for a month? No, Vacuum Square.
- Can I create a few extra hours of writing each week by eliminating another non-supportive activity? Yes, supports the #3 Goal.

Give it a try, and let me know how it goes for you!

Happiness is to enjoy an uncluttered life, happiness is to enjoy your own company AND the company of others, happiness is to enter calmly into the next week with ease and joy, happiness to me is to feel accomplished and productive, calm and caring, healing others. Being patient has not always been my strong point and the universe sends me hints and emotions to balance my growth and intention. Our own spirit does try to block anything uncomfortable and sends us along a path to offer a weary embrace. But it's time to work through and continue to evolve, rather than to arrive. Nourishing those activities while you are on your journey of life.

*****

"Be too busy working on your own grass to notice others may be greener or not." – Unknown, from gracemastered.com.

*****

<u>REVISIT</u>

A good morning routine with frequency sets our day for an abundant life. I heard that somewhere. Daily practices may not *seem* to be doing anything at the time, but let me explain what happened yesterday!

Backstory: Last week we liaised with our broker and real estate agent, and came out of that meeting very disheartened and quite upset. However, "PULL YOURSELF TOGETHER!" I chanted to myself. I meditated at a high frequency and took some time off the next day. I upscaled my morning routine to the frequency of abundance. A financial and physical 'pain-free' frequency played all day during my clinic hours (at 174 Hz, 555 Hz and 888 Hz) and I continued without thoughts more complicated than just to BE PRESENT in abundant energy for myself and those I was seeing during my day.

Which brings me to yesterday, when we received an email that said, CONGRATULATIONS!

We can now sign a contract for our new apartment, meaning that at the end of our day we will stay once a week at the Ocean International Hotel (so we don't have to drive all the way home to the beach house tired and monitoring our fatigue status), AND we were upgraded to the penthouse suite!

NOW – say that that isn't attracting abundance! And the only thing I had changed was my morning routine, revisiting my energy and my own frequency that I emit.

***

*"**Dear Monday, I want to break up. I'm seeing Tuesday and dreaming about Friday. Sincerely, it's not me – it's you.**"* – Authentically Del.

***

<u>YESTERDAY'S FLIGHT</u>

"Kids!" I repeatedly yell, now at a level that would wake the dead, "I don't know why you can't just wear your shoes like normal kids!" Having to go back into the house each time we get in the car. "I forgot my shoes," echoes the chorus from the backseat. "We are *never* going to make our flight," I choke out as I slam doors. "Angry!" sings the quartet in unison. Our magical relaxing family trip to Fiji – no doubt when we get there – will be the most relaxing thing I've done all year. The resort has a day spa, kids' club (which is what sold the whole thing to me), multiple restaurants and a 'parents' retreat delight'. YES PLEASE. But it seems the passage to get there will be paved with angst and complete stress. "It will be all worth it in the end," husband chimes in.

Arriving at the airport after we struggled off the international connection bus, nearly losing a foot on the bottom step while disembarking, the check-in queue was out the door. "I need a coffee," I said with heavy sigh while limping, pre-empting husband's sentiment, "Looks like you need a coffee, babe?" The café was closed for renovation; nevertheless, my stomach rumbled.

To get in the tropical spirit I had thought it would be a good idea to pack bright yellow matching shirts and yellow flower garlands, but my excitement to get into the Fijian mood had been met with scowling faces and 10 horrified eyes. Seeing as we had to be waiting in this queue, now sitting on our own suitcases, shoes being removed and then flung at each other, I extracted the 'surprise' – "SURPRISE!" I sang melodically. Our 16-year-old would have jumped into a grand crevasse if it would only have opened up right there in the airport. "There will be a beer in the departure lounge," I said to hubby, with the hope of cheering him up. "Come on, guys, just put them on?" I begged. The onlooking public laughed. Family obliged – eventually.

We finally got up to the check-in desk, and handed the staffer our IDs and printed tickets. "Welcome, Family Farraday, fabulous outfits!" There was then a considerable amount of typing and eyeballing. "I'm terribly sorry to inform you," said the puzzled-looking airline clerk, as we all stood holding our breath, like six little ducks all in a row with our yellow Hawaiian shirts and flower garlands, "but you are 24 hours late – your flight was yesterday!"

***

"Let's begin by taking a smallish nap or two." – A. A. Milne.

***

<u>SMILING</u>

Words are funny things. So are feelings, so is security, so is bliss, so is joy. What's really in it all? Are you important on your own island and your loved ones around you? Do you offer love and joy to all whom you meet during the day?

I do find all this puzzling in the sense of the word...LOVE.

In a biblical sense, LOVE is adhering to the Ten Commandments. To others, it may mean very different things – some emotions, some self-care, some even physical; to some it's security and the feeling of friendship, and simply to some it's happiness. In short, whatever LOVE is to you, wouldn't it be an amazing world if we respected ourselves on a personal level to LOVE whom we see in the mirror, to LOVE how we treated others, and to LOVE what we do all day?

So how can we live lovingly, daily?

To me, it seems simple. Let the light in. Inspiring stories and words of inspiration can let the light in, a hug can let the light in, a random act of kindness can let the light in, knowing you are a small fish in a big pond but there is love and support around you can let the light in.

So, I ask you, how can you let the light in daily to yourself and others too? How can you connect more with the energy of gratitude for yourself and others and kit out that big chunk of life that you struggle with within yourself, to embrace a connected and less-shaky ground? Create a sacred space of happiness for yourself and let your light shine as magnificent as you are!

It's A Connection We Can't Explain – So Get Lovin'!

***

"1. Going to bed early. 2. Not leaving my house. 3. Not going to a party. My childhood punishments have become my adult goals." – Dr. Dee Hacking.

***

THE ATTENBOROUGH FAN

Anthony grew up watching the nature shows each Sunday evening in the '80s. Such a special event – mother, father and Anthony all sat around the TV with great adulation for David Attenborough. Fast-forward 30 years and Attenborough is coming to town and Anthony has a ticket to see him on stage.

Anthony doesn't sleep well the night before; he sleeps poorly anyway. His thoughts dance from Emma – glad she is still safe on some home-soil base somewhere although he doesn't see her much these days – to the condition of his house, until finally, he fights off his grief. Sometimes he is able to press the thought of the baby out of his mind with a diligent focus, sometimes it is futile; the city seems to be full of dads with strollers, a haunt of what he is missing out on. He still remembers eating the strawberries from the garden before the baby died, he and Emma picking homegrown strawberries with little Amelia by their side. But now coming here to be solitary, he is cursed being alone with his thoughts. The garden plot though offered comfort, as he would see some tiny creature making its way over the soil and rocks and up a leaf, and in his mind he would adopt 'the Attenborough voice and lingo' and offer himself a running commentary, Attenborough-style, on the animal's adventure.

So now, he was off to the Sir David Attenborough event to elevate his spirits and to meet his idol. The 'Seven Worlds, One Planet' show was a mammoth event. *"This is where you come alive…"* the introduction song rang out through the auditorium and the thousands of fans roared and clapped, including Anthony. A whale sounded, then two whales, three whales all communicating with their pod, accompanied by graphics on the big screen – spectacular. Sir David spoke: "Listen to the sounds; the Earth is speaking." This opening sequence rocked Anthony to the core. He needed to listen, not to dwell inside his own grief destroying any sense of self that still existed. Sir David's presentation continued: "Thank you for being here. The oceans cover two-thirds of this planet of ours. There are seven great continents on which we human beings live; the liveable earth space is only one-third of the planet. These continents have their very own problems, as all humans have their own problems." Anthony was changed for life in those few moments.

At the end of the event, Sir David said, "One last thing tonight – I have someone special to introduce to you." He pointed into the crowd as a young woman walked out onto the stage. "I'd like to introduce you to this lovely lady." Anthony took notice, and froze. It was Emma standing up on stage. "There is a gentleman out there, his name is Anthony. Where are you, Anthony? Come up on stage." Then there stood Emma and Anthony, and a picture of Amelia was splashed up on the big screen, and the audience was presented with an exquisitely touching story of loss, hope and magic, and a reference to 'Sir David's mega-fan'. Such a beautiful thing for Emma to do for Anthony following his breakdown.

***

"I'm just the least funny person in a room full of funny people, which is basically every single day of work for me." – Ben Feldman.

***

<u>509 PACIFIC</u>

That was a wonderful summer of so many amazing memories. The house was built next to my childhood home. I never thought I would go back to the same neighborhood that I grew up in, but 509 Pacific is the most magical home I've ever lived in. It's not a typical New York apartment, for one main reason – it has a pool. I'm not aware of any other New York CBD home that has an outdoor pool in its own garden space.

Built in magnificent Petersen brick, my home combined sophistication and superior craftsmanship in the heart of Boerum Hill. My four-story condominium home is all about space, volume and massive proportions. My son once brought over his new girlfriend and their two friends. I instantly didn't like the pair of friends; he resembled a thug and she resembled a call girl (I didn't catch their actual names, but as far as I was concerned, I had named them!). They all got tipsy on my imported Champagne, smashed the wet bar on my rooftop space, then wanted to go for a swim. I certainly put a stop to it all, frustratedly asked them all to leave, and gave my son a big frown as they departed. "If you ever want to sell, we'll buy it!" slurred Harlot, as she stumbled and tripped down my front steps.

The summer came and went. I enjoyed many a sunset on the roof, soaking in the tub looking out over the Brooklyn skyline and its twinkling lights, and floating around in my little historic and rare pool. The winter was particularly cold, and the snow came for nearly the entire time between October and May, very unseasonable with intense blizzards, but it turns out I can hardly recall ANY of the winter now, as I float around in my pool blissfully. It seems all my memories have been deleted from my brain, from December onwards. I don't recall Christmas, or the holidays at all; must have been boring. The summer had definitely arrived though, and all I wanted to do was float around in my pool. I'm so lucky to have had the opportunity to retire and now just float – float for eternity looking up at the full moon, high in the daytime sky.

I watch the moon pass over the rooftops and skyline and pop out the other side. I've lost track of time as I float. I hear some noises, and giggling, and the clinking of glasses. Four people walk through my patio door and place their goodies on my sundeck chairs, place MY imported bottles of Champagne on the side tables. "HEY, HEY!" I shout at them, but they just ignore me. "ASHTON! WHAT ON EARTH?" I shout at my son and his awful friends. "I'll call the police!"

To my disgust, Harlot then strips completely naked under the failing light, and joins me in the pool.

"OH NO, NO YOU DONT!" I go up and splash her. My splashing doesn't deter her – she doesn't react at all, and I think she must already be very drunk (she had better not throw up in my pool…).

"Your mother would be missing this – it's so magical here, Ash," spits out Harlot.

"Gross, Delilah!" Thug shouts to her. "That's the same water she died in!" As if realizing a possible insensitivity, Thug continues, "So sorry for your loss again, Ash, but glad you let us move in with you. You need your friends right now, even though I think your mother would hate us being here all the time – she's probably turning in her grave…"

I continue to stare at them in silence, as they splash and shout, not reacting to me at all. Now I can make neither splash nor ripple in the pool. Harlot floats and floats, always naked, and always too close to me.

***

***"Some things are definitely better left unsaid, unfortunately, I often realise this after I've said them." – notsalmon.com.

***

<u>FAST, FLAT AND FUN</u>

Why do I do this to myself every year? The run nearly kills me, and my feet are unrecognisable under all the blisters, blackened toenails and blood-filled socks – but I love it. The Sunday morning is always hazier than any other day of the year. Not only the lactic acid build-up, but the celebrations that ensue post-race are unavoidable even when I promise myself, "I won't next year," but then I do it anyway.

'FAST, FLAT AND FUN' is the name of the fun-run; it's a fundraiser charity event for cancer research. It's anything but fast, anything but flat, and anything but fun. I feel personally compelled to do it, after the diagnosis of my sister, many friends and a colleague also, but each year I 'break' in the middle of the road race – always at the 26 km mark; why is that? Emotionally I'm a mess; my sister's spirit is there at the 26 km mark, my BFF is there at the 30 km mark, my ex-partner is there at the 36 km mark (all in situ), and I feel the symptoms of their fights – and their lost battles – right up to the finish line. I grieve each year at the same time; will it ever end?

A marathon is a long way, and a cancer journey is also a long way. My feet are numb, and my legs want to buckle. One of the most factual things about running the distance – the distance is never going to change. It's time to be the best prepared I can be on the day and the contentment on race day is vital. The demands of the marathon physically and psychologically, out there in the sun for such a long time… I'm specific with my training, but each year there's a different psychology of grief. This thing that is called 'post-trail depression' hits me early, even before the race is over. I'm shocked at how noisy the non-natural world is, realise how much 'stuff' I need to declutter in my life, and I find myself disgusted with the consumerism that surrounds me – the grief and loss for the sense of myself every year is tiring. Everything I hold dear is a big part of who I am, and now that I've started to lose each part of it bit-by-bit I don't know who I am anymore. Lots of questions arise, cluttering my head; existential worries that can be depressing.

After the race day is done, and I return to my natural world that is still under construction, my monkey-brain is not satisfied with my increasingly simplified life. It wants to make lots more decisions, looking for more purposeful actions, looking for adventure and community. I go online and read my horoscope, and it tells me that Cancerians have vivid imaginations, have great ambition, have boundless energy. That I like to travel, and I love the outdoors. That in loving relationships, I am sincere and whole-hearted and require the same in return. I decide that I need another Cancerian in my life.

Fast-forward to the 26 km mark the following year. I watch the distance and time clock over on my run-tracker. I feel strong and my breath is organised, not patchy; my head is clear, and I seem to be ahead of the other runners, no bottleneck congestion on the trail this year either. I feel an energy of victory in each cell of my body. I see a fellow runner, a runner that I've not seen before, and we are dressed nearly identically. "Hi!" I choke out. "Hi!" I get back with a nod. "Who are you?" I say as the next kilometre clocks over; we are shoulder to shoulder now, close, like running partners would position themselves.

"I'm a Cancerian," the other runner says, with a broad smile. I wink, and the rest is history.

We saved each other that day, and we continue to do so, for each day forward.

***

"ME: I want to travel more. BANK ACCOUNT: Like, to the park?" –
Anon.

***

JUST START

JUST START! I start every day by inspiring myself. I pick a card, from one of my many decks (one is a very special tarot deck handed down to me by Mum, that my grandmother originally bought for Mum MANY moons ago), offering myself direction, inspiration, and daily guidance – starting my day with sparkling energy!

This has been a family tradition.

I'm so glad I was raised with this intuitive, inspirational energy around me. Our children also have to be surrounded by this amazing ritual, and I text them each a card daily. It's a little gift I'm happy to share with others, too, choosing a card for them; such a nice little surprise to offer to people to start their day.

Yesterday a friend and client of mine sent me a card that she had chosen for me, which deeply resonated with me and set me to putting my energy into the message.

"Weaving your dreams into the fabric of life begins with a single thread of intention," reads the Spider Spirit card from the Oracle Deck. "Make your dreams real."

I couldn't have said it better myself! This is like my little life's motto – *find the little gems within each day by creating your own happiness* – a very similar message that I live by daily.

The Spider Spirit message continues by suggesting taking a single step to making your dreams a reality and being the co-weaver; the universe is designed to support your dream-weaving. "Ideas and resources will magically appear; something tangible comes from creativity. Practical thinking, visualising, writing, painting, journalling, gardening. Let yourself be open to abundance." *THERE IT IS!*

WHAT COULD YOU DO TODAY TO WEAVE YOUR DREAMS AND GOALS INTO TODAY, AND EACH DAY?

- Just start.
- Tiny steps.
- Don't compare yourself to others.
- Get creative! Write, paint, garden, journal, visualise the END RESULT in YOU!
- Live the dream NOW and let abundance do the rest. EASY, right?
- JUST START!

***

"I read recipes the same way I read science fiction. I get to the end and say to myself, 'Well, that's not going to happen.'" – Rita Rudner.

***

<u>THE CEO</u>

Whatever it is you do, be a product of your own product.

There's a hierarchy in life, yes, I'm sure we are all aware. Quite a natural hierarchy of existence, like survival-of-the-fittest, top-of-the-food-chain style, so in your work and business it's easy to default to hierarchical thinking and actions.

This kind of thinking will have you at the bottom – every time.

Shining when you're at the bottom is insanely difficult with so many above you; mindset is a strange thing. It's also difficult to shine when your energy is flat, even if you are at the top of the business food chain.

So when is it your time to shine? Most will say...when you've done the time! But it's time to change regular thought patterns and ask yourself, "What would I be doing if I were my own CEO of my life?" Decide to position yourself as your own authority, creating the mindset to back yourself to your own success and believing that NOW is your time to shine. Shine in your own authenticity and remain within your own vibes. We humans tend to like to look abroad and mirror ourselves off others, looking to the top for inspiration, so pull yourself up and just be yourself and shine within your own space on your own board of directors.

So how do you back yourself and position yourself to be your own leader?

- Planning time. Set intention. Plan for a good plan. Get a diary. Plan for your work for sure, but also plan IN YOUR DIARY for exercise time, meditation time, self-learning time, reading time, embrace your passions time... For those 'little' things are the most important – trust me.

- Personal development and improving yourself. Just 30 minutes a day. Nourish yourself. Personal investment.

- Daily actions towards your goals and dreams.

- Connect with other like-minded people. Humans perform better in groups – we are 'community' people.

- Cultivate the expectation of leadership. Co-host, write, blog, put yourself out there, look out for your own personal health and wellbeing. BE A PRODUCT OF YOUR OWN PRODUCT. What is it you do – be that person. Offer gratitude as regularly through your day as you can, and HAVE FUN. Find a way to make it fun. "If it's not fun, it won't be done."

- Be in the here and now. Mindfulness. Work within the moment of energy – this will prevent linear overthinking.

Keep a little check on yourself as your own CEO, by performing self-evaluation with *constructive* energy, not 'self-bashing' energy. Is it your time to shine now? ABSOLUTELY.

Please feel free to connect with me (my socials are on page 155 of this book) – I would love to hear from you. I work with individuals all over the world and assist them within their own energy too.

Decide where to position yourself by being the CEO of your own life.

***

"I stopped buying women's magazines. The only time I ever see someone who looks like me is under the word, 'Before.'" – Sarah Millican.

***

THE DETAILS

The Devil is hidden in the details, or is it the MAGIC that is hidden?

I sit here in my little home office. Calmly. Music playing. Candle gently burning, offering the room coconut and vanilla scents. I type and gaze out of my window into the rainforest at the back of our beach house. Sand out the front, bird-filled forest out the back. Heavenly! I feel the magic here, within these little details. Hectic day planned? YES! Those to whom I will speak today on my business calls, no doubt the same as the people I spoke to yesterday within online meetings and consultations, will hear the joy in my voice, experience my calm demeanour, and see on the video calls how 'magical' my life is.

It's all within the little details – there lies the magic.

I look up from my laptop and view my list of goals Blu-Tacked to the wall. A new list of goals it is, as my previous goals I have attained and ticked off. The life I now live is a far cry from my reality only two years ago. Stressed out running three busy medical clinics in two different Australian states, 14-hour workdays six days a week, and no space to enjoy my passions, or even my family. Yet the strong desire to attain time-freedom, physical health and to work from this magical home full-time radiated from within me. The magic is in the details. I could, and did, visualise daily my 'now' life. Details. Little tiny daily details I would include. I then became that person now by adding the 'future me' details into the person I was at the time. With the will and goals strong enough, you can make it happen no matter what.

I meditate at sunrise each morning on the beach; other people now join me and state what a wonderful life this is. It sure is! I'm filled with gratitude right at that very moment. I am now busy creating the further 'future me' details and inserting them into my daily life so that I am now on the way to my NEW future self and ticking the goals off, step-by-step, on the new list that is now hanging on my wall within my view. I am visualising myself in two years' time, reflecting upon this very moment sitting here typing, and taking note of each little magical detail, for it isn't the Devil but the magic to our own successes!

***

"The walk you do in the shoe shop before you buy the shoes, your own impersonation of yourself, and pressing the big toes in the shoe for no reason at all, you will never EVER walk like that again for the entire life of the shoes." – Michael McIntyre.

***

THE LETTER

A letter for me arrived in the post today. I recognised the handwriting; it was mine.

I had totally forgotten about the letter I had written from a TEDx talk here in Mackay over 12 months ago. My brain was usually like an elephant's brain, but not today, and I rushed to open the letter to see what on Earth I had had to say for myself last year!

"You are Wonder Woman!" I had written on the lined page. "Your past obstacles have designed a new strength for you to now pave the way, just GO FOR IT. I'll be there to celebrate on the other side." Myself, telling ME. GREAT advice. Still a surprise!

This had made my day. I felt pumped and excited and ready for the

MAGIC to happen.

Even for the assertive and confident and outgoing, all this is not a foolproof remedy against self-criticism and self-doubt. Recently within my personal development endeavours and continued self-education, I came across the 'multiplicity me' scenario, a theory which I had also forgotten about. It was like the 1996 science-fiction movie 'Multiplicity' starring Michael Keaton. I recall that the movie was about cloning, but I don't exactly mean cloning – instead, I mean multiple YOUs in all areas of your life. The many echoes of yourself that follow you around all day. The you-echo in the morning before coffee, the you-echo that goes for the sunrise walk, the one that is rushing and commencing the day, the you working, the you on lunch-break talking to others around you, the you that's late for yoga class, the you that is yet again rushing to make dinner, the hungry you-echo making coffee again as you did in the morning, the you reading a book to wind down, the you who is totally exhausted at the end of the day. Do you like and trust the many YOUs? Did you all sit quietly on the yoga mat in the class, or did you argue and banter back and forth? Did you all sigh with happiness in unison with that delightful first sip of coffee? Is it time to reconnect to EVERY ONE of YOU? Be harmonious throughout your day? Do you allow your past struggles to guide and strengthen you, or do you hijack your own happiness?

My little thought-catalogue from 12 months ago continued to highlight that no doubt I'd be doing really well compared to then – recovering from a heart attack and a fractured knee, I HAD to be on the upward scale from there, and I had had the realisation, with a panicked undertone, that I could not go back to doing the 80-hour weeks on my feet in my clinics that was my prior life grinding me away to a shadow of myself.

I am super-excited to say I had come full circle within that year. So many obstacles, yes, but also so many new ways of overcoming obstacles, and so many lessons learned. My energised Wonder Woman self was back, vibrant and sparkling and finding the little gems within each day – now as a full-time transformation coach, author and entrepreneur (as my letter had insightfully suggested!). I HAD MADE IT to what and where my previous 12-month-ago me had wanted future me to be!

Thoughts do really become things.

What will *your* "Dear ME" letter look like?

Wonder if I should write a letter to my ten-year future self now?

***

"Adventures always come to the adventurous, there's no doubt about that!" – Enid Blyton.

***

POWER CARDS

I start each day of my life by choosing a card. Always have.

When I was a small child, my mother Marie and I would choose a card daily and read the little messages to each other, and wish each other a magical day. One summer, during my school holidays in 1981, Mum and I took a set of cards up to Grandma's house in the country, and she thought that we were both mad! She didn't believe in any of this 'doing the cards' or 'wishing each other a good day', because every day was a 'struggle', she said.

Not too long after this, Grandma came into Melbourne by train, and Mum and I met her for a luncheon at the old Spencer Street Station (now a much-expanded complex, and renamed Southern Cross Station). Grandma announced that she had a special gift for us. It was a 'Renaissance Tarot Deck', printed in Switzerland with French titles (Mum had spent some time in France in her youth, and holds anything French dear to her heart!), with mythical Greek deities of Olympus. It's a beautiful deck. Mum totally loved it, and Grandma announced, "Let's do the cards!" So we all chose a card each, read them to each other, and wished each other a sparkling day.

Mum gifted me the set of cards when I last went to visit her this year. It was an amazing surprise, as I had not recalled them during the subsequent 40+ years since the luncheon day! Mum and I then spoke fondly of the luncheon with Grandma at the station's restaurant, and Mum was surprised I could remember all the little details from that far back! Mum and I then each picked a card and read its message to Grandma, who is no longer with us, as she passed not long after that special luncheon date.

I had commenced the little card tradition with my own two children when they were young. We would all choose a Power Thought card from a Louise L. Hay deck of cards and read the little meanings to each other and wish each other a magical day. My kids have now grown up and moved out, but I SMS them the cards I still choose for them daily. They love it, too; they say it offers them gratitude and guidance to start their days. And this tradition is even more special to us since we have started using Grandma's set of cards, with its box now taped up due to its age and worn spots.

Never stop believing! Little miracles happen every day. Start with a Power Thought card, gratitude and a little self-guidance. Why not?

I sit here reading the message from the Magician card. I have recently randomly selected the Magician card from four different card decks daily. As I was selecting from Grandma's deck just now I accidentally knocked a special little book off a bookshelf in my office, and a loose page has fallen out…it's the page for 'The Magician'…

I'M LISTENING…

The Magician has all the elements in front of him, embracing the Jungian belief of intuition, feelings, thinking and sensation with everything he needs to succeed, and is well connected. He stands upon a rich garden filled with flourishing flowering plants. His clothing depicts his purposeful activity, pure intentions and aspirations with infinity of spirit and manner. Thank you for this inspirational energy: TODAY I ENTER THE DAY WITH THE ENERGY OF THE MAGICIAN. I receive the message being presented to me, and I send it back out into the universe, and it all makes so much sense in my life currently.

So why not commence your days wishing yourself a sparkling day, practising a little self-guidance, embracing gratitude, and enjoying an inspirational message? And offer it all to others around you, too? The repetitive processes may just sift out the clumps of negative energy that seem to build up in all of us, and may even offer us a reminder during our hectic days to retain the positive energy and to keep connected to ourselves and our journeys.

***

***"Great things often start off small." – Roald Dahl.

***

CANCEL MONDAY, AND GO BACK TO BED

"I've cancelled Monday, go back to bed!" JACKPOT!

As I cruise through Pinterest on the search for motivation (and the next popular hashtag!), I remind myself: attitude, energy and strength. These are my superpowers. The realisation was actually transformational. And powerful, yes, but I'm still allowed to 'cancel Monday'!

Discovering your powers can be a huge realisation that sets you on a different path. Focus your powers directly towards your goals and allow your specific attention to be directed and supported by your powers.

In my authentically 'me' fashion, I ask, "What would Wonder Woman do?" I often pose this question to myself, to motivate myself to find a solution to my challenges, problems and daily duties that need pondering, then actioning. This question is written on both our kitchen calendar and my vision board. "What would Wonder Woman do?" Always a great fan of magic, superheroes and superpowers, I do believe we all have our own superpowers that if we tapped into them, we could lead the fulfilled life that we desire so much.

At school I would sit up the front in class, pay great attention, work for top marks and pressure myself into perfectionism. In one class, to my great surprise, I was told I had a bad attitude. The teacher isolated me from the rest of the class as it was 'out of character' as I usually made it my position to motivate my peers, maintaining electric energy and strength, and people usually wanted to be around me, to siphon my electric and positive energy. My 'bad attitude' was the result of my not liking the class and its content – ATTITUDE. It was many years later that I came to recognise and control both my powers, though not yet realising at this point the full magnitude of my future discovery. My newly discovered 'control' increased my energy even further and a domino effect was set in motion, running my strength and attitude on a continual forward and recharging motion; in turn again, more energy.

Do you charge yourself as much as you charge your phone? I've always been a big fan of personal development and as the years passed, I worked on myself via physical exercise, yoga, metaphysical work and discipline, emotional and mental work and great study too – to become a doctor, homeopathy and injury specialist, and leader in my professional field. I used to think that 'energy vampires' would seek me out and surround me, sapping my electric energy and depleting me. Then it hit me, attitude and strength ARE my energy, and energy is everything. THIS IS MY STRENGTH. Like that of Wonder Woman: strength, attitude, energy. My Wonder Woman arms raise in a cross in the air.

"You are stronger than you believe. You have greater powers than you know." – Antiope to Diana, 'Wonder Woman' (movie, 2017).

AND ONE DAY I DISCOVERED MY POWERS. The *magnitude* of my powers. So what did we then DO with our power? For me? To 'bring it' by me, for me, then for my family and our desired lifestyle, and for others. Giving is the biggest gift of all. If I undermine my own strength and attitude, then I'm 'hijacked'. More power, to 'bring it' for my health, via great planning and daily steps; for my online business yet again via great planning and daily steps; for my finances AGAIN via great planning and daily action; for my family again via continual planning and organising events. Don't compare yourself when you are at your page ten to another's page 60! Use your superpowers to embrace your energy, learn to elevate your own energy, and then utilise your powers to do constructive work daily towards your goals and vision and for others. The process on paper seems like an easy equation, THEN life gets in the way. Therefore, Plan B and Plan C to combat life's hijacks are also imperative. Formulating good solid plans eases the pain of the prospect of 'quitting'! With consistency and effort, the difficulties of the process towards your vision will abate. Times will definitely be hard, and life can be exceptionally challenging, but are you prepared to roll up your sleeves and 'bring it' and exercise your inner strength?

WHAT'S YOUR POWER?

***

"Thank goodness we are us; be no one else." – Marie A. Elson.

***

<u>THE INGREDIENTS</u>

Ingredients combine together to result in a delectable portion of delightfulness. If an ingredient is missing, then the entire recipe may very well crumble and be a total mess. Self-criticism, negative internal dialogue and constant vocalising of what you perceive as your worst and most dramatic problems, all train your brain and your body, and ultimately your life, to become something you don't want to be: anxious, stressed, and depressed. Continually overthinking and vocalising your problems in the negative to pretty much anyone at all, is the greatest addiction plaguing humanity that is usually overlooked. You are unknowingly digging your own hole!

"Self-talk is the most powerful form of communication because it either empowers you or it defeats you." – Wright Thurston.

And if it defeats you, it can do so SILENTLY. So what is the missing ingredient in our lives for our own happiness and contentment if we participate in continually self-talking in the negative?

To be aware and to realise the enormity of one's own thoughts, sometimes one has to be either superhuman, a psychologist, or an enlightened spiritualist. Most of us aren't any of those. Spoken and unspoken words can either be influencing or damaging, right? Don't allow your lower self to take over. Okay, so how do we do that?

Are you willing to get out of your comfort zone? See yourself for what you are? Most will say no to all this because the space in which you usually exist has been constructed to either protect yourself or to live comfortably, without a great deal of fear and doubt, as really all we all want is to be happy and safe. However, there is no personal advantage here, we need to continually learn, be the student. Once you get into doing it, it will flow and you will learn when you need to recognise to not fall into the old thought patterns. Odds are, you too have listened to others talking in the negative – how do you handle that? A friend may express to you many pitfalls of their lives, the latest family issue, the negative chatter of crumbling relationships; your energy drains just listening to it all and you find it even more draining computing it internally. Would you rather be you, or an echo of yourself which is exactly what one becomes after continual negative chatter?

Don't sell yourself short, this is not a time for that. In leadership, business, and marketing we are to build a tribe, understand our tribe's present pain and problems, create a solution/assist them to find a solution for themselves, assist in the solution where necessary and implementation of it, then amplify, then allow forward growth.

How? The buzzwords around are to practise positive self-talk – do your thoughts build you up or tear you down? Enhance your functioning or hijack you? When you listen to your inner monologue are you surprised at how harsh you are on yourself? *"Whatever you believe on the inside is what you will manifest on the outside."* If you are constantly talking about your problems and putting yourself down, how will you ever be the best version of yourself?

A directive to 'practise positive self-talk daily' is simply reframing the negative thoughts into a more positive nature-boosting self-confidence, self-awareness and self-belief, while not listening to other people's opinions of you. Propagate words that are non-judgemental and non-critical and that offer joy to yourself throughout the day and towards others. NO WORDS OF COMPLAINTS! The inner critic has now gone on vacation.

TIPS TO COMBAT NEGATIVE SELF-TALK:-

- Speak to yourself with compassion. You will do better and keep moving forward. Just ask yourself the questions: "What more can I be doing to help myself and not hinder myself? What can I be learning from this situation?"

- Break the habit of self-complaint and complaining to others. Bring awareness to your thoughts and replies. When you start paying attention you may be surprised at how much you say in the negative. Remember that your subconscious is internalising this and manifesting this.

- Journalling and checking your environment. Cut back on fear-based news and 'doomscrolling' altogether. Clean and declutter the house. Surround yourself with positive people and like-minded individuals who do positive things, rather than engaging in negative cycles of behaviour.

- Challenge your belief and comfort zones. Remember that not all thoughts are actually true. Create a calm space between you and your reactions. Don't just automatically accept what you think, and then say it.
  "Whether you think you can or you think you can't, you're right."
  – Henry Ford.

- Choose. You have the power to choose your reaction. Choose one thought over another, and act in the positive.

- Do daily practice. The truth is that we all feel negative emotions. But it's a choice whether to engage or not, and a choice to take little action steps daily. A bodybuilder doesn't win the competition on his first day, but with continual work and focus, the bodybuilder can win any battle.

- The missing ingredient. After asking yourself, "How can I learn from this? What's the lesson here?" the missing ingredient is your tolerating what you attract. What you tolerate you become. The ingredient is within your mind to go from a 'chase' focus to an 'attract' realm.

- "I am no longer going to have any toxic behaviours or toxic words in my life." This is a starting point. Self-commitment. Most of us are quite accepting of our own and other people's toxic behaviours. STOP. We attract what we tolerate. Set boundaries. Don't feed toxicity in any fashion. Create distance, recognise your own toxic behaviours and set about addressing them. Trust that things will get better. Reflect and make yourself accountable. THEN, celebrate each win. No longer just accept the negative.

***

"The energy that defines worlds and creates universes is within you."
– Dr. Wayne Dyer.

***

PICK A DATE

For a moment let's visit the ideal of success, and success at whatever you are needing to accomplish for the day. Let's look at success as a pathway and lifestyle rather than a destination. If we are viewing from this standpoint, then three quick ways to beat procrastination will involve making changes to the way we do things. It's not about motivation at all, it's about being inspired in that moment to NOT procrastinate, but just DO.

- Do what you like doing the least, first. The things we tend to put off are the things we like doing the least. For me, this has been making particular phone calls – would you believe it? As an extrovert and medical professional, I usually have zero issues talking to people about any subject, but in THIS instance, fright and flight sets in. THE TIME IS NOW, COUNT DOWN AND DIAL AND SPEAK. After about 20-odd calls, and yes making an ASS of myself, no problem at all. Why did I procrastinate?

- Make your goal bigger than your excuse. Eyes on the prize, peeps! The courage to really go after your goals will be found by squashing all the procrastinating mind-chatter. Picture yourself IN and LIVING your desired goal and all other ideas and thoughts will be sidelined.

- Get ready to celebrate your win. There is nothing better than a celebration. A WOOHOO moment, a good old fist-pump in the air. Organise your reward. It may be as simple as a nice relaxing bubble bath; if so, go purchase the luxurious celebratory bath solutions and essential oils of your choice. Pop them in a prominent location and then give the plan a measure, AKA timeframe. "I *am* going to take my celebratory bath on…" and pick a date. Then, develop and formulate a plan so you will arrive at that date with completion.

Procrastination is out the window, and you are on track! Keep on track, and don't let yourself hijack or punish yourself unnecessarily.

***

"To succeed in life, you need three things: a wishbone, a backbone and a funny bone." – Reba McEntire.

***

THE SHIPWRECK

You can definitely wreck yourself and beach yourself daily, weekly or annually too. Or, be like our Harry and Spice (our dearly departed Dalmatian dogs). Harry used to love sitting awkwardly on top of Spice, like she was his own personal couch – was he wrecking his day, or hers, or both?

It can be quite a challenge to survive your own life, each day with pain and misfortunes, to advance to happiness and land on the beach whole.

We do know that each obstacle we overcome makes us stronger and wiser. You will heal and grow, but HOW exactly to take little steps to keep going in that septic moment? It's a constant fight for happiness, right?

- Identify the feeling. Stop yourself from indulging in previously destructive thought patterns and crankiness, recognise and squash those destructive actions you have previously allowed to shipwreck yourself.

- Music. Sing or listen to something ASAP. What's your favourite song? Or, what's your 'vision song'? Do you have one? The song you will play when you have reached all your goal milestones? My favourite is Beethoven's Moonlight Sonata No. 14, I play it daily to avoid shipwrecking myself – it's amazing the abundance that follows once you allow it.

- You have the power to influence. You have the power to influence yourself, others and the energy around you. Influence the room. Watch out for being a negative, shipwrecking influence on others, and watch out for the shipwrecking energy of others being a negative influence on you. BE THE POWER THAT INFLUENCES FOR POSITIVE ABUNDANCE.

With awareness comes clarity.

With action comes change.

With influence comes personal abundance.

A friend of mine did a survey just this week on defining wealth. It turns out that 'wealth' to MOST participants of the survey (including myself) was initially defined to be money, and then having 'stuff' was included, but then in ALL consideration, true wealth was found lying within daily gratitude, love for yourself and others, and energy we possess and give back.

Interesting, isn't it?

So maybe, just maybe, surviving our own personal shipwrecks offers love, gratitude and energy to those around us, our family members and those who enter and go within our days. REAL wealth.

"Actually, I'm a bit of a sucker for second chances. They're my first favourite kind of chance." – New Girl (2011).

<u>IT WAS THERE ALL ALONG</u>

Say it and live it like it's already done. You've had it inside you all along, did you know?

Your true self is saying that you are thriving, but what you think about is what you end up manifesting. You are never too old, or too stuck, or too far gone, or too broke to dream a new dream, to set another goal and create change. YOUR GOAL. Say it and LIVE it like it's actually DONE! The realisation will hit you, clarity arrives, and a clear pathway will become visible and ready for your action. The path won't be easy but it's visible and actionable. LIVE LIKE YOU HAVE ARRIVED and you will arrive! It's all inside you, now just use it!

Like wearing sharp clothing, a new well-cut dress, a well-fitting suit, you love the flattering style and the bold, vibrantly alive print. You feel confident and strong, you are standing tall, you talk to yourself in the mirror, "You're lookin' fab today!" You KNOW today is different from all the other days.

You walk outside and slide into your imaginary Mercedes-AMG, and the aroma of the leather interior fills your nostrils. Your drive into town from the beach is clear and easy even after the monsoonal rains. Unlike your usual mundane arrival in your dusty old Ford and parking way at the back, you secure a front-door arrival in 'your AMG', hand the keys to the valet and shimmer as you stride inside. You arrive on the third floor, exiting the lift, unexpectedly greeted with, "You are all dressed for today's occasion, how did you know?" You're presented nicely at your shimmering best, and you are handed all of a promotion, a glass of Champagne and a company car. Not just any company car, the boss's 'old' AMG as she is receiving her new one. SAY IT, LIVE IT, WORK

IT AS IF IT'S ALREADY YOUR REALITY. Is willpower a limited resource for you? Willpower is a mode of self-control within the short term, to then gain in the long term. Attitude. Attitude is the key. Attitude, choices and effort. Radiate energy, radiate positivity, and then anything is possible. How do you action all of this? Forget just positive thinking. For years, self-help gurus have been suggesting positive thinking is the answer to all. However, if you truly want to improve your life you have to literally change the core way you think, not just your thought patterns. Force yourself – say it and live it like it's already done. I CAN, I WILL – WATCH ME! A sentiment I've always lived with, I adopted this as a young child and my mother recounts numerous 'defiant' and 'willpower' stories of mine. I CAN, I WILL. AND WATCH ME.

It's time to start telling the universe what you really do want, not what you don't want, and to start living like you have already got it. You didn't wake up today to be average or to have a bad day. Our mental chatter is a self-fulfilling prophecy, so feed it wisely with both your goals and your end results in clear view.

Go for your dreams! Find a way to achieve them, or make one!

***

"As long as you're going to be thinking anyway, think big." – Donald Trump.

***

EVERYTHING WORKS

"Everything in my life works for me, for now and evermore, I say 'OUT' to every negative thought. No person, place or thing has power over me." – Louise L. Hay.

Why is it we all seem to enjoy the weekends more than weekdays? The answer is seemingly obvious. More down-time than work time, the schedule may not be as intense as the weekly working days, and inclusive of being our relaxed self: "Just being YOU!"

There are four simple steps you can implement daily to fall in love with each day and actually enjoy your day no matter what the schedule looks like, negating the dreaded feeling that leaches in and hijacks you before you have even started.

- Keep a check of your feelings. Stop yourself. Own the intention of 'being you', choose your thoughts and feelings to adjust to the state of LOVING YOUR DAY. We are continually receiving incoming information, and the power for you is to choose how you react and how this affects your feelings.

- Set your intention. "Today, I prosper wherever I turn." Have a self-propelling positivist mantra on hand. Repeat it every hour or so if needed.

- Search for the FUN in it all. If it's not fun it won't be done. Do what you have to do and invent fun ways to complete each daily task.

- Enliven your imagination and learn one new thing per day. Do you have core interests, hobbies, creative prowess? This is the magic dust. Enlist yourself to liven your imagination and look forward to something awesome that you love, daily. This may even be watching something on YouTube in a field of interest to you. Learn a new skill or even something you've been planning to do for years and haven't. Keep it simple and workable, but keep it daily. This will all add up to feelings of self-achievement and will raise your energy and vibration.

I have always commenced my day by choosing a card. I have boxes of Power Thought cards, tarot cards and the like and as my kids were growing up, it was a special morning moment to start our day, choosing a card each with a daily message to be received. Even as they have grown up and are living their own lives, I still choose a card and now SMS it to them to keep the tradition and positive daily momentum flowing. At first they had thought I was quite mad, but they grew to love it, and if I happen to miss a day they message me with, "What happened today, Mum?"

Just be you. Love each day. You are enough. Live lovingly towards yourself and others.

***

"I believe when you put a smile out there, you get a smile back." –
Heidi Klum.

***

<u>START AGAIN</u>

We all have moments in our lives that demand us to have courage, strength and our full attention. The static of the world fades away and we arrive in our own silence; often for most people, an uncomfortable zone to be in. Painful are the lost moments, in whatever form they take – maybe a word unspoken now regretfully paused, an action silenced by our own self-talk, motivation that fell away, or times of frustration gagged by rage. We are confronted with the enormity of that lost moment and the possible results 'if we had continued', becoming the observer in fast-forward in this unfulfilled experience, and moving into a deep awareness of how things could have been different or how they really are now! Standing in the ashes of our plans is ultimately difficult, and often met with personal disdain and hostility, resulting in our own side-effects. We will never be immune to all the changes and lost moments that we experience.

So, what do we do? The lost moments I'm referring to are the moments where our brain, our internal world, hijacks our plans and stops us. These are the lost moments when regret sets in and the seeds of defeatism start to germinate. The moment, for example, where I sit with my daily planner looking upon my strict plans directly in front of me; my required phone script, phone, laptop, all open on the corresponding pages, stepping my brain 'outside the box' from my comfort zone to make my 50-call list, a new field outside of my chosen career. My soul panics. Panicking about the 'new' tasks to do, the possible conversations and problems I may have to address, the simple fear of not knowing what personality or who will be on the other end of the line. *STOP!* That's what my mind says. My inward voice then argues with my actions and halts my progress. I even count myself into the action, 5-4-3-2-1 CALL, but then hang up before my prospect answers. I get up and walk away. From motivation to sudden defeat. Two hours later I sit with regret looking at my phone and my abandoned 'to-do' list and see a pile of failure. The self-talk turns to motivation to start over. "Get GUTSY!" I chant to myself. "I can and I WILL." Take a breath, and another… After dealing with all 50 calls, I breathe another deep breath, and acknowledge a moment of success, and it actually wasn't so bad. Repetition and consistency, and fast-forward five months and my daily calls are no longer hijacked – with a little personal grit, there is no longer another lost moment.

HOW-TO: How to work through the defeatism mindset. You must have a clear view of your end targeted result. What is it that you are doing and what is the best desired outcome? THE GOAL? Stop overthinking about what you are supposed to do and be flexible and open to your own compromise, put 'all your eggs in one basket', hone in on the activation of the task and GO FOR IT; be flexible to start over if you panic. Take a breath, and start over immediately. We are not falling victim to the building process that starts to gradually descend into a series of mini-defeats and mini-hijackings, you will construct a false sense of reality for yourself and have a 'fake success'. The difference? The end result! Reaching your goal for the task. And then? NEXT!

It's up to YOU! There is no one coming to either do it for you or to rescue you. Pick yourself up, dust yourself off, and start again. NEVER feel guilty for starting again. And count each win!

"What you know matters, but who we are matters more while you are finding what you know." – Brené Brown.

THE WORLD IS MORE BEAUTIFUL WITH YOU

When you find yourself alone with your thoughts…

Most people have an abundance of pleasant, often joyous, and fun thoughts, BUT when we find ourselves alone with our thoughts, unpleasant or even painful thoughts can creep in and take a stand at the front. We have worries about unresolved problems or upcoming stresses, memories of difficult or embarrassing experiences, angry thoughts about unfair situations, and sad thoughts about disappointments, losses, and endless 'to-do' lists. Thoughts of panic ("I can't do this!"), thoughts of failure. Overthinking. Stress. Fatigue. Anxious moments. Can you see the unravelling nature of this mental ripple effect?

Mindfulness, a word a little overused in recent times, in my opinion, yet I also think it has a true place to stand. Mindfulness provides a new perspective on thoughts. Mindfulness of thoughts means that we now are aware and watching these thoughts come and go with friendly curiosity and non-judgemental acceptance. If we view our thoughts as a spectator sport, we allow ourselves to remain in control and in turn will not allow ourselves to hijack our life towards a septic field. When you are mindful of your thoughts, you realise that thoughts are continually appearing and disappearing and that you can choose whether to believe and comply, or dismiss and move on. We do try very hard to distract ourselves with things like excessive eating, drinking, partying, shopping; but this doesn't ease anything, it just leads us down a destructive path of ill-health, negativity, and depression, and this is a compounding effect.

Why is it so difficult for us to be alone with our thoughts? Because we don't like facing ourselves. The human mind is more comfortable focussing outwardly; yet true growth, healing, happiness and contentment arrive when we work on ourselves and our thoughts and go within. Working within, on a daily basis, I find that for all of myself and my clients and business associates, using personal development techniques teaches us the processes to adjust and control our thoughts and in turn our spoken words, behaviour, health, lifestyle, relationships…and ultimately our success in achieving an optimistic and inner-directed positive outcome.

Unfortunately, it's not a case of flicking a switch and having puppies and rainbows arrive for your daily pleasure. It's hard work, but the world is more beautiful with you and your positive, radiant energy of a focussed mind filled with purposeful thoughts!

***

"There are few things in life that are harder to find and more important to keep than love. Well, love and a birth certificate." –
Barack Obama.

***

<u>TWENTY YEARS OLDER</u>

Old age is always 20 years older than I am, that's for sure!

Now let's be honest. We are guilty of saying, "Oh, I'm too old for that," or "I'm simply just getting too old!" We all do it (if you haven't – yet – just give it time!), whether it be as a cop-out, or as an excuse for our memory, physical ability or lack thereof, or simply a refusal to get the job done. Raise your hand too if you are guilty! I know I am. I was so kindly informed by a dear friend of mine, that when I turned 40, it was the new 20, so chin up! When I hit 45, I found that old karate and dance injuries plagued me, and new injuries appear due to me being unstable on my feet from the previously mentioned, and advancing arthritis. A requirement for surgical intervention saw the surgeon's line of enquiry aiming for a conclusion about the extent to which he was going to repair my knees: "What are your future goals – do they include triathlons or hiking, or just simply the ability to walk?" WOW! My mental state went from rock-around-the-clock to limp-around-the-block. My blunt self-assessment was that I'm old enough not to feel youthful anymore but young enough to still want to participate fully in life, yet now must I limit my future lifestyle due to my physical parts. All I know is that I AM ENOUGH and I'M TRUSTING THE TIMING OF MY LIFE! That's it. So from here on in, the creaky neck, times of immobility, heel spurs, body aches, insomniac nights, capitulation and joint noises must all arrive with a sprinkle of optimism. I'm not too old for anything, I AM ME. Time to change my life and mindset around to embrace 'The Vibrant Me'! As C. S. Lewis said, "You are never too old to set another goal or to dream a new dream."

- Life is a series of tiny gems – notice them! We cannot become what we want when we remain exactly what we are. Are you an enthusiast in life or are you riding the wave with blinkers on in a mundane existence? I've realised how important it is to notice all the little things, the beauty that surrounds us, and to be actually involved in them too – life is not a spectator sport. Embrace the magnificent process; hug it, love it, and above all become passionate about it. What is the simple thing that makes the happy people of the world so happy? Awareness and savouring – noticing a thing or moment, stopping, pausing and savouring that one moment a little longer. Simple. Attention and intention.

- Think before you speak. Be the reason someone smiles. To speak before you think is just plain hurtful in most cases. In this current sociological environment we are taught to openly communicate and express ourselves to the nth degree, yet I'm sure this intent was not meant to be 'free speaking no matter what the content or consequences'. We humans are often very hurtful towards each other, so a little forethought might be the answer to our future selves' physical health, mental health, happiness and personal vision for the future. Open your mind before you open your mouth!

- Choose to prosper. Don't be afraid to give up the good and instead go for the great and the fabulous! Believe in the person you are, and the person you want to become. It can be quite off-putting if we are not guaranteed comfort and security, so we remain reluctant to engage as we need to. Let's get to a deeper level. Anchor yourself in the future. I often ask clients how they see their future self, what vision do they have for themselves and their lifestyle. Often they have not even given it a thought and have zero idea, then they will always strike the mark! It's hard to let go of the past in the absence of a positive view of tomorrow. You need a vision for the future. Choose a good self-investment, choose to PROSPER and not merely exist. With a spark of excitement to set your soul on fire, something ahead will then supply you with the energy necessary to catapult you forward. Any person who contributes to prosperity will then prosper in return.

Let's ask again. Are you too old to trust the timing of your life? Age is a journey, experience is the vessel, and vision is your future and lets us know the happiness that time brings, by not counting the years.

***

"Friendship is born at that moment when one person says to another, 'What! You too? I thought I was the only one.'" – C. S. Lewis.

***

LIVING PROOF

Is this really where you want to be? Stuck? Well, it is what it is, but the power of detachment creates your new normal. Shoot forward but get yanked back via a contraction, so sever the attachment and forward you shall go again.

Until I grasped this concept, I remained STUCK in my 'fabulous' life I had created for myself. Successful in all that I did, I dealt with my personal challenges successfully also, yet was the delivery and the lifestyle that which I desired, or what I hoped to be working towards? That was a huge NO!

I implemented a few personal development strategies and ADDED to my life with the intention of creating SOME minimal change towards my desired life of my dreams. ADDED, but then created a large contraction worse than I had experienced previously. It was a contraction of ill-health, professional disaster, financial stress and personal stress. This could have stopped me for sure, but NO! What did I do? Readjusted, readjusted, and made more readjustment, all over time…to total CHANGE. If nothing changes, nothing changes. GOT IT, FINALLY.

Working in the personal development arena highlights that my ultimate goals need to be the critical drivers. I was trapped within the wheel of day-to-day functioning and working myself to exhaustion daily (looking back now, I should have stopped myself). Ultimately, where do I want to be? NOT STUCK, NOT IN THE RAT RACE, that's for sure. Recently playing the game of CASHFLOW® by Robert Kiyosaki also highlighted how easy it is to be lost in your own momentum with your dreams and goals still present, visible, and tangible, but not attainable via the current actions. Until I took specific planned action to get my feet on the ground and made the connection and traction – moving forward is the key, yes little by little with consistent effort.

IF NOTHING CHANGES, NOTHING WILL CHANGE.

Navigate the terrain, keep it together, tune out of the negative mind and actions, and keep going within your critical drivers towards your own qualification of your dreams. It is possible. I'm living proof.

***

"I'm sorry captain, he called 'shotgun'…got us on a technicality!"
Always keep your words appropriate. – Anon.

***

DON'T TRIP OVER WHAT'S BEHIND YOU

"Thank you, NEXT!" These three words continue to resonate and bounce around in my head. These are three powerful words that gain momentum the more I ponder. "Don't trip over what's behind you!" also holds hands with these three words of great personal interest. It wasn't until I was presented with a patient's troubles in my clinic that I found myself delivering all of these words to my patient in one long line. It was the light-bulb moment for both of us, and an energetic cloud of realisation filled the room with an air of total satisfaction. "That's IT!" my patient exclaimed, "Don't trip over what's behind me, THANK YOU, NEXT!" and she left with a renewed zest to clear out the past and be excited about her NEXT for her future. Simply let go, and action the new.

Energy and zest. Motivation at its finest, in my opinion. I was recently asked what 'lights me up'. Without a second to rethink, I started replying. What motivates me and excites me to do the things that I do? I gratefully have a long list and continue to reply without pause. Thoughts creep in from the past and make me question, "Am I worth it? Of course I am," I reply to myself. I am enough. You are enough.

I didn't come this far to just come this far. Follow your course until success. Rule your mind or it will rule you. Sometimes we do struggle with the past. From mistakes, to regrets, to reliving bad habits, negative déjà vu, anger, frustrations, lost loves, relationship changes, physical pains and hurt. What if we could actually have the past remain in the past, and live a happy life? What if, with a loving act, we could all move forward with zest without tripping up and letting the past events sabotage all of the wonderful times we are in store for?

Dear 2019 Self: *Don't get worked up over things that are both out of your control and that is someone else's opinion.* Things definitely don't just disappear; working through the past is a very important skill. Many differing things in life can trip us up, and expressing ourselves is vital to remove the pain. Disconnecting from it, then realising you are no longer the same as when this happened to you, then making room for the new. No doubt one of the hardest lessons to learn is the act of letting go, truly letting go. Change is never easy. You may hold on to a fight, but letting up is generally the healthiest and most rewarding path forward. Let go of things you don't need that cause drama and distress, hardship and ill health.

TIPS TO CENTRE YOURSELF:-

- So I've personally come to realise it's not about 'getting over it' or 'JUST working through it', it's about coping and KEEPING GOING. This little quote of my mother's resonated with me even as a young girl: "Accept what is, let go of what was, and have faith while creating a pathway to what will be; trust in your journey." I've had this written in my gratitude journey, vision board and kitchen calendar as a daily reminder for years!

- Practise thinking better about yourself. Time to quit belittling yourself, being angry with yourself and thinking that you're not enough. Come out from the façade of smiles into a 'reality' of seeing things differently. Face yourself in the mirror daily and repeat a positive affirmation that resonates with you. Your mind is where the battle is!

- Embrace the fact that you are MORE than what has broken you, or what hijacked you! When times are tough, little pieces of us break off, chipped away from our soul and happiness. Realise that you are more than the sum of your parts! We usually have an idea of our ideal us, ideal life, IDEAL me. Picture that and head towards it. You are not just one thing, you are many things, so BE MANY, stretch and change your identity, BE THE FABULOUS YOU. Shine and sparkle in your authenticity.

- Change and evolve. Start over again, and again, if needed. I've heard many times people say, "Starting over is not an option!" WHY NOT? This is a lie most of us hold on to. You can change paths as many times as you like! No one wins a game of chess by only moving forwards – moving both sideways and even backwards puts you in a winning position. Count your daily wins and learn from your setbacks and changes.

From now on, what should you do? Something small, baby steps, plan, be clear on the goals you have and your purpose. LET GO AND GROW. No pits of despair, commit to a bright future, give yourself a challenge, set your course. Rule your mind and when a memory surfaces, concentrate on not letting your past influence your future and control your fate.

"It is not in the stars to hold our destiny but in ourselves." – William Shakespeare.

***

"Always try to keep the number of landings you make equal to the number of take-offs you've made." – Aviation in a nutshell.

***

BE THANKFUL THAT YOU DIDN'T GIVE UP

The time will arrive; you are now very thankful that you didn't give up. You've experienced the excitement, "I can do this!" This then travelled into, "Is this worth it?" to arrive at the regretfully painful, "I've made a bad decision," but your inner voice tells you, "You've come this far," and demands you to keep going. You repeat mantras (because you are a positive person and you won't give up, from all the hurdles and failures and endless mental chatter battles). The universe is responding to who you are and shifting things in your favour. You are attracting abundance in all positive arenas, practising gratitude and now finally you are Thankful That You Didn't Give Up! So what's the secret? Your vision and efforts come down to one thing – INTENTION WITH AUTHENTICITY. What is your WHY? If your WHY is strong enough, you will figure out the HOW issues.

I always WIN! Commence. Give it a go. Succeed, fail, learn, fail, learn again. Go. Go. Succeed. Win. NEXT. AND REPEAT.

That is my learning and personal experience of the cycle. Ups and downs, disappointments, excitements and frustrations inclusive. If you continue to count your wins from every lesson presented, there isn't any room for 'failure', there is always a WIN. Challenges along the way? Absolutely! More often than not, all the time! However, it's your ability to adapt, learn and follow your ultimate intention. What are you actually doing this for? What's the goal? Do you actually see yourself living and loving the end result or is it a 'hollow goal'? Just words written to somewhat motivate you? Do you really inspire yourself? It's time to get REAL with yourself and embrace your authenticity.

Genuine. Honest. Authentic. All rare. Why? So many of us today ultimately despise the FAKE and augmented reality, yet still seem to mirror what others do and present, knowing all the time that in this modern world transparency is highlighted! To be open, honest and true, I've seen individuals inadvertently create a false sense of authenticity; both external and internal, roadblocks stand in the way of becoming truly authentic. Their constructed world becomes less authentic in reality. Viewed from an external position as FEAR and LIES! Constructs built to avoid others, and others' opinions, yet in the long term, there are things on the list that have that same effect they are trying to avoid. SO, it's okay to stand up and be yourself. We relish those stories of celebrities who struggled before becoming incredibly successful. How J. K. Rowling was living on welfare when she wrote Harry Potter, former teacher with a small child at home; how Richard Branson struggled with dyslexia; how Stephen King's first novel was rejected 30 times before finding a publisher. We eat up these stories because they emanate authenticity. I bet too they are glad they didn't give up! We aren't perfect ourselves and we aren't perfect in others' eyes either, so don't be afraid to be imperfect, truthful, authentic and REAL in all your glory!

Are you Thankful That You Didn't Give Up? Life and the duties of life can be so overwhelming, I know all about this in my busy clinical practice and as a business owner too. Stop trying to 'be like them', it's all about planning. Become a strategist for yourself. Reduce your duties to 'baby steps' planning for every hour of the day; have a plan B strategy. WHEN it all goes off course, then plan again, your plan B kicks in and you're not then overly stressed about the change. Reassess, don't let life hijack you, and keep going. Tick off a job or duty, NEXT. Simple...and don't give up on yourself, BE YOU. Your strength is that you are not perfect and that's what's going to make you stand out!

So, ask yourself the question: "Am I thankful that I didn't give up?"

***

"I don't make the rules, ma'am, I just think them up and write them down." – South Park (1997).

***

DINOSAUR (A 3-MINUTE TALE)

A fallen tree sits on our beach at Ball Bay, near Mackay, Queensland. Not just any fallen tree; it's a true curiosity. A magical being etched at daily by the lashing waves, gnarled at by other driftwood of its kind, and with an array of aquatic creatures in residence. Barnacles, nestling starfish, and hermit crabs occupy its casting shade. It is regularly sat on by the land-dwellers, and visited and sniffed at daily by the photograph-seekers and their canine companions. Here lies the 'Ball Bay Beach Dinosaur' – he's no actual dinosaur, just a large fallen tree. A loved, iconic structure discarded by the sea, a dear friend to many locals, and a delight of discovery to holidaymakers. He listens to all the confessions whispered by passers-by at daybreak, to the heavy exhale of the sundown beach joggers, to the soft chatter of the dog-walkers, and he even sits quietly as the canines drench his popular sniffed areas.

Walk, and the way shall appear.

You are unaware of the existence of the Dinosaur until you start walking down the beach. He sits at the far end of the beach, down where the crocodile slides. Our sand is fine and silica-based (great for shining your jewellery); soldier crabs eagerly create their little balls of sand and scatter away as you approach; shells litter the beach, and as you look up, there he is! He awaits your arrival to hear your confessions, lift your spirits, and send you off with great clarity after the counselling session.

As you walk, the way does appear.

You have destressed, and you now know what to do to figure out your problems. You realise that if you 'do the same things daily' and expect different results, you're mad! Your steps are more rapid as you return to your natural life off the beach with renewed vigour. Rain and shine, the Dinosaur is waiting like a BFF. A training partner who is waiting on the beach for boot camp. He knows that to succeed in life, you must put your health first. It's not about being selfish; it's about taking pride and concern for your physical and mental state and creating a balance. The daily workout consists of activities for daily and future success, daily 'I AM' affirmations delivered with a vibrancy to set up your future self and attainment of goals, plus push-ups, sit-ups, walking, swimming, and yoga poses.

Accountability. Daily steps forward.

Today, I discovered our friend half-buried!

The wild full moon tide had dumped tonnes of sand, and the feeling of 'a friend half-buried' stabbed at my heart. No shells, no hermit crabs; the urchins all buried or departed with the outgoing tide, as are the starfish. The shore is silent. The Dinosaur is silent, too.

As I do each day, I walked, and how I appeared changed. My life and mind change daily; stresses and schedules come and go as the tides do, and sand is dumped unexpectedly, covering up all the beautiful things and emotional riches. Do we dig and grind away and work so hard to unearth ourselves and return to the same as we were before? Or do we accept change and new beauty? Do we panic, become saddened, and even angry at the rest of the world, blaming the world around us? Or do we still be quiet in our minds, accept the change and what's in front of us, and work towards different results?

I patted our dear beach confidant as I was leaving to return to my natural environment off the beach; I informed him of his beauty and announced my intended arrival tomorrow morning.

Today, I also reached one of my personal and health goals and even pushed through to change my schedule to commence my next 30-day plan to focus on my goals and execute my well-formulated plan to tap into my full potential.

I then realised it was the first of the month, August 1st. Powerful.

With great gratitude, I found our Ball Bay Beach Dinosaur half-buried today!

Start to walk, and the way appears.

No walk – no realisations, no action.

How often do you think about a better life for yourself? You've worked this hard, and is this all you have? You are SICK of the struggle, the shortage of time and cash. Tired and frustrated with areas of your life and feel personally disconnected and dissatisfied? The question really is: "How do I get from where I am to where I really want to be? To be happy, content, and balanced in all areas of my life?" On no planning, no daily steps.

The answer is self-love. It's quite as you may expect. It's not about LOVING everything about yourself and being 'perfect', and it's not as difficult as you may expect. Self-love is not about looking in the mirror and chanting words back at yourself; it's workable and enjoyable; you will be astounded at the results, how quickly you feel better about yourself and your life, and how action can change your situation dramatically. Energy is everything. The energy and vibrations you emit when you are frustrated, tired, disconnected, and dissatisfied are exactly the vibrations you get back from the universe. So, let's now alter all of THAT to elicit powerful energy that will, in return, bring you success, prosperity, abundance, and balance.

Think about 'choosing the colour of your lens' – consider a traffic signal analogy.

Let's say for a minute that you get to be in charge of the metering system that sets the traffic lights. You get to choose when they flash from red to amber to green. What if you could decide how to colour your life? What mix of colours would you want at any one time?

Begin to practise these three easy steps to learn how to colour your world the way you want!

- Start to notice the colour of your thoughts.
- Be aware at any moment of which colours you are creating. You may need to learn to run some red lights first!
- Practise changing the lens and move from red to amber, then amber to green.

***

"If you are the kind of person who is waiting for the 'right' thing to happen, you might wait for a long time. It's like waiting for all the traffic lights to be green for five miles before starting the trip." –
Robert Kiyosaki.

***

Other Publications by Dr. Dee Hacking

SPRUIK IT!: Cultivating the Willingness to Back Yourself to Your Success. Barnes and Noble, 2022. LivingLovingly Press. USA.

The New Rules of Wellness: Transformational Stories from Health Experts Who Lead from the Heart. House of Wellness Publishing, 2023. Australia.

The New Rules of Wellness: Transformational Stories from Health Experts Who Lead from the Heart. Volume 2. House of Wellness Publishing, 2024. Australia.

Change Makers: 21 Transformational Stories from Women Making an Impact in the Lives of Others. Co-author. Change Maker Press, 2020. Australia.

Voices of Impact: Empowering Stories From Female Visionaries and Entrepreneurs. Co-author. Voices of Impact Publishing, 2022. Australia.

More. A collection of short stories (Volume 2). House of Wellness Publishing, 2024 release. Australia.

The Doorway. A collection of short stories (Volume 3). House of Wellness Publishing, 2025 release. Australia.

Aurelia's Tide: A Novel. House of Wellness Publishing, 2025 release. Australia.

Connection: Phil Andrade (Wildcard)

Please connect with our friend, Phil Andrade – musician and band, **Wildcard**.

@wildcardthedragon on socials.

Find his new album *Western Promises* at www.wildcardqm.com

Find his song 'Death Card' (as referenced in the stories in this book) on YouTube at https://www.youtube.com/watch?v=AVLBiQJD9X8

Author's Message and Thanks

You made it to the end of my little collection! I hope you had as much fun reading my stories as I did writing them. More to come!

Thank you to my existing followers and fans who have been with me for a while. Your ongoing support means the world to me. And a big hello to my new fans, and thank you for checking out my book – I hope you and I will continue to be friends for a long time to come.

Thank you to Phil Andrade for song lyrics and collaboration. Thank you to A. W. D. McIntosh (FWC) for editorial assistance.

To my wonderful husband John, our beloved children, and our dear extended family and friends, just – thank you.

Please connect with me on my socials below to talk about the book, life, the universe…and anything and everything! Would love to see you there.

XXXX Dee

Email: houseofwellnesspublishing@gmail.com
Facebook: https://www.facebook.com/nereda.hacking
LinkedIn: Dr. Dee Hacking

Publisher's Message (Get in Touch!)

House of Wellness Publishing is a boutique publisher created and run by Dr. Dee Hacking. Its purpose is spreading true tales of health, wellness and inspiration, along with stories of fiction (including novels and short story collections), and so much MORE!

Dr. Dee originally hails from Melbourne, Australia, but for many years has made her home in the Queensland coastal town of Mackay, where she runs her own highly regarded health clinic (*Bay Massage & Homeopathy Allied Health Clinic - Dr. Dee)* as well as her publishing business.

Dr. Dee is already a bestselling author in the fields of health and wellness, and is delighted to now be publishing her first volume of short fiction with **A Clue to the Invisible Pyramid**. Stay tuned for more!

- If it is also your dream to be a published author, perhaps you have something you would like to talk about with Dr. Dee? She would love to hear from you via her socials. Even if you don't think you have something to say **about** wellness, there's a very broad spectrum of subjects and stories that could help **promote** wellness in our readers, so let's have a chat!

House of Wellness Publishing is the originator of the international bestselling **The New Rules of Wellness** (NROW) series. You can find the published NROW volumes on Amazon. ***Author submissions for chapters in our upcoming NROW volumes are currently open (2024-2025)*** – please contact us via the **email** in our socials to discuss.

Socials:
Please see page 155.

www.ingramcontent.com/pod-product-compliance
Lightning Source LLC
Chambersburg PA
CBHW071924130726

47909CB00014B/2575